TROUBLESHOOTERS

Skye Fargo and Angus McCord were a good team. But with the gang of killers they were up against, they had to be perfect.

Angus was a blink faster than the one who fell backward, the hole in his heart gushing blood. Still, another gunslinger managed to put a bullet into McCord's upper left arm before crumbling, with one of Fargo's bullets in his head. Unnerved, another member of the gang missed his chance and McCord got him in the gut.

Fargo exchanged shots with the man closest to him and managed to tear the right side of his skull off.

Finally, the last guy left dropped his gun. "Don't kill me!" he pleaded. McCord calmly ignored him.

Five men dead should have been the end of trouble. Trouble was, it was only the beginning. . . .

GUNSMOKE GULCH

by

Jon Sharpe

A SIGNET BOOK

SIGNET
Published by the Penguin Group
Penguin Books USA Inc., 375 Hudson Street,
New York, New York 10014, U.S.A.
Penguin Books Ltd, 27 Wrights Lane,
London W8 5TZ, England
Penguin Books Australia Ltd, Ringwood,
Victoria, Australia
Penguin Books Canada Ltd, 2801 John Street,
Markham, Ontario, Canada L3R 1B4
Penguin Books (N.Z.) Ltd, 182–190 Wairau Road,
Auckland 10, New Zealand

Penguin Books Ltd, Registered Offices:
Harmondsworth, Middlesex, England

First published by Signet, an imprint of New American Library, a division of Penguin Books USA Inc.

First Printing, November, 1990
10 9 8 7 6 5 4 3 2 1

The first chapter of this book previously appeared in *Sierra Shoot-out,* the one hundred sixth volume in this series.

 REGISTERED TRADEMARK—MARCA REGISTRADA

Printed in the United States of America

PUBLISHER'S NOTE
This is a work of fiction. Names, characters, places, and incidents either are the product of the author's imagination or are used fictitiously, and any resemblance to actual persons, living or dead, events, or locales is entirely coincidental.

The Trailsman

Beginnings . . . they bend the tree and they mark the man. Skye Fargo was born when he was eighteen. Terror was his midwife, vengeance his first cry. Killing spawned Skye Fargo, ruthless, cold-blooded murder. Out of the acrid smoke of gunpowder still hanging in the air, he rose, cried out a promise never forgotten.

The Trailsman, they began to call him, all across the West: searcher, scout, hunter, the man who could see where others only looked, his skills for hire but not his soul, the man who lived each day to the fullest, yet trailed each tomorrow. Skye Fargo, the Trailsman, the seeker who could take the wildness of a land and the wanting of a woman and make them his own.

*Summer, 1860, in Colorado high country,
where a treacherous woman and worse men
were brought together at the end of a rainbow
and sweet revenge came quick . . .*

1

The big man astride the powerful black-and-white pinto stallion dug a silver compact out of his pocket. He had taken it from Marie Mercier's clothing. The Louisiana whore's naked dead body lay where it had fallen in the Mexico desert far behind him, a victim of the Sharps, but not by his hand. Flipping the compact's lid open, he studied the length and shape of his mustache and beard in the tiny mirror. Skye Fargo decided both were all right. He snapped the lid shut and returned the compact to his pocket. The piece of jewelry was destined to belong to Miss Candy, who owned the saloon at Wagon Wheel Gap in Colorado. Candace liked to receive gifts, especially jewelry.

Fargo was headed due north, riding under a warm sun. He was about ten miles inside New Mexico Territory, on the rutted trail that passed Clearview Hill. Atop the lonely hill one could see for miles. He decided to go up it and look around, stretch the kinks out of his muscular body, and let the stallion graze.

Facing south, the rise offered him a majestic panoramic view of a vast expanse of the raw and still untamed territory. Although it was a sunny day, he saw storm clouds building in the west.

Skye Fargo would be gone before the storm struck. He would be on the trail followed by wagon trains heading north to Beaver Pond in Colorado Territory. He whistled for the Ovaro, which had gone down the rise to graze. The stallion came immediately, with his ears perked.

"Good boy," Fargo whispered, rubbing the pinto's face. "Time for us to be moving on."

He eased up into the saddle and put the pinto at a

walk. He passed the time by counting how many wagons left the fresh ruts. He concluded that seven Conestogas had made them.

Soon the scenery changed, to Fargo's liking. A stream off to his left gurgled as it rushed south over a rocky bottom; a woodpecker drilled for a worm in a dead tree; six doe, followed by the buck, crossed the trail ahead. He was in the mountains, in a narrow valley; blue spruce were everywhere as far as the eye could see, interrupted by slashes of golden aspen, their leaves quaking in the gentle breeze. An unseen elk whistled.

Rounding a bend, Fargo's wild-creature hearing detected a new sound, one that didn't belong to nature. He nudged the Ovaro to lope and went to investigate.

In a small meadow were seven Conestogas, all overturned, six still smoldering. Bodies littered the ground. All had arrows in them. Riding in, Fargo heard a pain-filled groan. He dismounted instantly and began a search.

Coming to the overturned Conestoga that had not been torched, he spotted an old man sitting on the ground, his back against the wagon's underside. Three arrows protruded out of the old-timer's chest. The man's eyes were closed and he was mumbling incoherently between pain-racked groans.

Fargo squatted next to him. In a flick of his eye he noted the depth and placement of the arrows. Fargo knew the tough old man was close to taking his last breath.

When Fargo coughed, the man's eyelids fluttered partway open, and he said with much effort, "The savage bastards took my Annie."

Looking around at the bodies, Fargo nodded. The old man found the strength to grasp Fargo's shirt and pull him nearer, then he whispered, "Find her, mister . . . find her. I'll pay you to find my Annie."

Releasing the shirt, his hands moved slowly to his own shirt pocket. The old man fumbled a small leather bag out of it, saying, "Open it, and you will see."

Fargo released the drawstring and dumped four nice-sized gold nuggets into his palm. He fingered them, looked at the old man, and asked, "What's your name, old-timer? Where did you get the nuggets?"

He wanted to ask more, but the old man cut him off. "Name's Roscoe Hogg. I got them from our mine, Charlie's and my mine. Charlie, he's my brother. The savages killed him." Roscoe paused to cough. Fargo heard a death rattle. Roscoe went on. "Find Annie, and take her to the mine. Annie will pay you ten times this amount. Promise me you will find her." He started coughing again.

Fargo had to wait for Roscoe's coughing seizure to pass, then said, "I'll do my best to find her, I promise I will."

The old man relaxed, closed his eyes, and died.

Fargo looked at the arrows, which he recognized as being Apache. He thought it odd their being in Colorado Territory, especially this close to the little town of Beaver Pond. He broke off one of the fletches and put it in his shirt pocket. Rising, he looked at the bodies again, then stepped to each. He counted seven men and four youngsters—three boys and a small girl—and two older women. He thought that odd, too, and went back and looked at the men's faces. Most were young. He guessed about twenty-five or so, no more than thirty.

Only one survivor, he told himself. Why did they take her? He looked at the old man and wondered if Roscoe had been mistaken. As far as Fargo and Hogg knew, Annie's body was one of the older women's. Hogg hadn't mentioned her age, whether or not Annie was his wife.

Fargo decided a promise was a promise. He would look for Annie. He picked up where the Apaches had left the massacre site easy enough and whistled the Ovaro to him. While waiting for him, the Trailsman counted many unshod hoofprints, among which were five shod. He thought that odd, too, and squinted to inspect the five. He concluded their depth meant only one thing: double riders. They had taken five women.

Mounting up, he began tracking the savages. They had gone west, crossed the main trail, and then turned south at a gallop. He found where the unshod ponies and the shod parted. The unshod riders went due south, the shod southwest. All led to New Mexico Territory. Fargo chose to follow the shod. After riding a short distance he found a piece of yellow gingham snagged on a thicket. Now convinced that they had captured women, he quickened the pinto's pace.

The first few drops of rain were big and cold. They dimpled the dry soil, but not enough to stop Fargo. Shortly the squall line unleashed its full fury, heralded by stiff wind, lightning, and thunder. He watched the shod tracks disappear as the earth turned to mud. Further tracking was impossible. He turned and headed back to the massacre site.

He rode out of the squall a short distance later and found the meadow as dry as before. He dismounted and located a pick and shovel in one of the wagons. In an hour he had dug a shallow, common grave to hold the bodies. After lowering them into the grave, he put the shovel to work and covered them up. Leaning on the shovel's handle, he removed his hat and muttered, "Rest in peace."

Grim-faced, Fargo put on his hat, then got in the saddle. Facing south, he saw that half the sky was solid black with roiling storm clouds. The sky above him was clear. A warm sun beamed down on the big man as he cut between two of the overturned wagons and headed for Beaver Pond.

Crossing the meadow, he saw shod hoofprints where none should have been. He followed them to a stand of aspens that formed the tree line on the northern perimeter of the meadow. Just inside the grove there was a knoll. On top of it he saw where a rider had joined up with seven others, all riding shod horses. The seven came from the direction of Beaver Pond. He followed their tracks down the rise. At the bottom, on bare earth, he saw a horse had thrown its left rear shoe.

Fargo proceeded to track the seven all the way to Beaver Pond, where the print of the horse with the missing shoe vanished among the many other hoofprints and wagon ruts.

He halted and sat easy in the saddle while looking down the one street of Beaver Pond. The little town had grown since he'd last seen it. He saw big Angus McCord's Trading Post was still standing, its sod-and-timber roof and log sides still in the process of rotting. One end of the roof sagged dangerously low.

Angus was the original inhabitant. The crusty, outspoken mountain man had named the place after the abundance of beavers' ponds in the area. Then he promptly killed all the beavers for their pelts.

In time, Bo Weathers built a small saloon facing McCord's place, just so they would have a street. McCord made Bo take it down and move it back aways, claiming all the noise bothered his "peace and tranquillity." Bo had no idea what tranquillity meant, but wasn't about to argue with the rough-cut mountain man. Bo moved the structure.

Fargo saw the saloon had been widened to twice its original size. In addition to front windows, it now had a high false front with the new owner's name painted on it in big white letters: SALOON AND GAMBLING HALL, JACK CASTLE, PROPRIETOR.

A small hotel named Beaver Pond Hotel had also been erected since Fargo was last here. A fifty-foot gap separated the hotel from McCord's Trading Post.

And there was a blacksmith's place, complete with a livery, next to the saloon. Fargo heard the smithy pounding on an anvil, shattering McCord's peace and tranquillity.

Next to the livery stood a feed store, with several Studebaker farm wagons parked in front. Adjacent to the feed store was a small general store, and next to it a new sheriff's office and jail. They have need of a jail? Fargo thought.

Fargo checked inside McCord's Trading Post and found it deserted. A few items hung on the walls, and the tables were filled with hides. Evidence that Angus was nearby. He looked at the horses hitched to rails in front of the saloon and walked the pinto over to them. He loose-reined the stallion to the rail, then began lifting the horses' left hind hooves. After finding all of them shod, he stepped to the swinging doors and paused to look inside.

Five men were seated around a table in the back corner, talking in low tones while sharing two bottles of whiskey from which they swigged often.

Six men stood at the bar, which ran the length of the saloon, each resting a boot on the wooden rail. A weasel-faced bartender stood behind the bar, wiping glasses.

Two other men occupied a table next to a window.

Nobody was gambling.

Fargo pushed through the double doors and moved to the end of the bar, where it turned and blocked access to the liquor, where he could see everybody in the room. "Bartender, send down a bottle of bourbon," Fargo told him.

Instead, the man himself brought the bottle. Setting it in front of Fargo, he said, "That'll be two dollars." He held out one hand for the money, kept a grip on the bottle with the other.

Fargo asked, "Two dollars? What's in it? Gold dust?"

Weasel Face looked at him impatiently and replied, "Two bucks, stranger. Take it or leave it."

Fargo's right hand shot to the man's shirt. Pulling him nose to nose, Fargo slapped two silver dollars on top of the counter and growled, "I'm paying, but I don't like your attitude. Give me another of your snotty looks or tell me to 'take it or leave it' and I'll drag you over this counter and beat the shit out of you. Got that?"

Weasel Face gulped and nodded.

Fargo let go of the shirt and swilled from the bottle. The men at the bar ceased conversing and looked at Fargo. During the silence the Trailsman moved to stand at the far end of the bar. Looking at their reflections in the mirror, he studied the men at the table in the back corner. Four wore ripped and torn dusters, and they had unkempt hair and hands, wild looks in their eyes. Drifters, he decided, the very kind who would kill their mothers for a nickel. The fifth man, shorter than the others, and older, was baldheaded and clean-shaven. He wore Levi's and a checked shirt that appeared clean. A Joslyn army revolver rode low in the holster tied to his left thigh.

Fargo's wild-creature hearing eavesdropped on their conversation. Baldy was saying, "You Barrow brothers did a fine job. Perfect, in fact. And I won't forget it."

Fargo watched them rise, shake hands, and heard the

older Barrow say, "Money talks. We'll be there to help. Won't we, John?" He cut his eyes to John.

John answered, smiling, "You said it, Neal. What our big brother says goes for all of us. Right, Ray?" John glanced at the youngest man. "Right, Frank?" He poked the other man's arm.

"Fine," Baldy said. "Then let's head northwest."

As they were leaving, Fargo turned and rested his back up against the edge of the bar. In a loud voice, he said, "You men wait up."

They stopped in midstrides. Neal Barrow turned to face Fargo and motioned his brothers to spread out. Pulling his duster open, Neal's right hand settled in position to draw the Navy Colt from its holster.

Fargo's elbows were on the bartop, the bottle in his gun hand. Grinning, he raised both hands and said, "I'm not looking for trouble. I'm looking for help."

As he spoke, a man entered through the back door and stepped to the bar. He was followed closely by a skinny, stringy-haired brunette with sad-looking eyes. She wore a much-used and abused, tight-fitting dress. She glanced at Fargo and shot him a halfhearted smile, then proceeded to go behind the bar.

Fargo continued, "What I was about to say was, I came across a wagon train about five miles from here. Apaches massacred most of the people." He pulled the fletched part of the arrow from his shirt and laid it on the bar to show evidence. During his brief pause, in his peripheral vision he saw the bartender hurry out the back door. "Young children and older women were also killed. But I know the Apaches took at least five females with them when they headed south to New Mexico Territory."

"How do you know that?" Baldy asked.

"Because I tracked five sets of shod hoofprints. All five horses were carrying extra weight."

Neal Barrow chuckled. "That don't mean nothing. Ever hear of fat Apaches?" Neal's hand released the edge of his duster.

"Only thing is," Fargo began, "there was a survivor, an old coot—"

"His name?" Baldy interrupted.

"Roscoe Hogg," Fargo answered. "I found him dying. The tough old buzzard had three arrows in his chest, any one of which should have killed him instantly. Just before he died, he told me his name and that the Apaches had taken his Annie. So I know they took her and probably other females."

"What prevented you from tracking them into New Mexico Territory?" the barrel-chested man at the table next to the window asked. "By the way, my name's Jack Castle. I own the saloon."

Fargo nodded, then said, "Look outside and you'll see what stopped me. Rain washed away all signs of their tracks. I'm going back to search for the women. I'm asking for help. If we spread out where the rain halted me, the hunt for them will go much faster. Can I count all of you in on this?"

"Er, what else did the old man say before he died?" Baldy asked.

Fargo had a funny feeling about Baldy, spawned when he preceded the question with the "er." It was time for Fargo to hold back information. He said, "Not much. Like I said, I got to him as he was taking his dying breaths. He did mention that the savages killed his brother, Charlie, too. Other than that, he was concerned about Annie."

Baldy visibly relaxed.

Fargo was about to mention the other survivor who met seven riders on the knoll. Before he could say anything, two powerfully built men came through the double doors followed by Weasel Face, who pointed a wavering finger at Fargo and said, "That's him, Sheriff. He's the one causing trouble."

Both the sheriff and his deputy drew their revolvers and aimed them at Fargo's chest. The sheriff snarled, "You're under arrest. Disturbing the peace in this town is a hanging offense."

2

Baldy and the Barrow brothers backed slowly to the wall opposite the bar.

"I'll get the rope," Weasel Face shouted, and ran outside.

"Come away from the bar with your hands up," the sheriff ordered. "Move slow, real slow," he added.

Fargo stepped away and faced the pair of lawmen.

"Disturbing the peace?" the saloon girl asked. "He wasn't—"

"Shut up, Melba," the deputy interrupted.

"Start walking," the sheriff ordered Fargo.

The deputy moved to one side to allow Fargo passage, relieved him of his Colt, then covered him from his backside.

The sheriff backed through the double doors and held one open for Fargo.

Fargo stepped through them. He felt cold steel press instantly against his back. Nudging him with the gun's barrel, the deputy grunted, "Across the street. Head for the jail."

Walking toward it, Fargo spoke for the first time since the lawmen's appearance. "What're your names? If I'm going to catch hemp fever, I'd like to know who I caught it from."

After a few paces, the sheriff told him, "I'm Buck Ott. My deputy's Silas Ferguson."

Fargo had heard the names before, in Wichita. Buck and Silas, he recalled, were killers. The worst kind. They gunned down five unarmed men in a saloon after one caught them cheating in a game of five-card draw.

As they came to the jail, Fargo saw the weasel-faced

bartender toss a rope over a sturdy oak tree limb next to the small building.

The bartender called to them, " 'Bout ready to hang him, fellows. Soon as I make the noose you'll get yours, you big son of a bitch."

"After I have my supper," Buck called back. He opened the door and went inside.

Evening's shadows, compounded by approaching dark clouds, spilled through the doorway as Fargo entered the small room.

Ott lit a lamp on his desk, then said, "Better search this one, Silas. I'll keep him covered."

Silas pulled out Fargo's shirttail, felt around his waist, and said, "No hideout or pocket pistols, Buck."

"Check in his boots," Buck suggested.

Silas found the stiletto. Holding it in the lamplight, he grinned and said, "Well, looky here. The fucker had an Arkansas toothpick." Squinting at Fargo, he added, "You figuring on stabbing my ass, huh, big boy?"

Silas' big fist powered against Fargo's abdomen. He saw it coming and flexed. The fist met pure hard muscle. Fargo just looked at Silas' puzzled expression and winked.

Ott said, "Leave him be, Silas, and lock the bastard up. Not that it matters, stranger, but what's your name? I like to know who I hang."

"Skye Fargo."

"I've heard of you. Aren't you also called the Trailsman?"

"I answer to it."

"Well, I do declare," Silas chortled. "We caught ourselves a real prize, didn't we, Buck?"

Buck grunted, "Lock him up, and we'll go eat."

Silas shoved Fargo through the open door to the cell, a continuation of the room, albeit divided by iron bars. Locking the door, Silas said, "Gonna be nice, riding that magnificent black-and-white stallion of yours hitched outside the saloon. He is yours, ain't he? Nobody 'round here has a horse like him."

Ignoring Silas' remarks about the Ovaro, Fargo lay on the bunk, put his hands under his head, and closed his eyes. He heard Silas snarl, "I'm gonna enjoy hearing your neck bone crack, watching your sorry ass twitching."

"Come on," Buck told him. "I'm hungry."

Fargo listened to the front door open and close. Opening his eyes, he stood and started testing the cell for security. The oak walls were sound, as was the ceiling. And the bars were solid. Standing by them, he looked at his Colt and stiletto on Ott's desk, so close but so far away. He lay on the bunk again, to think his way out of the windowless structure while listening to lightning rip the clouds and thunder that boomed and shook the building.

Raindrops pattered on the roof, then, shortly thereafter, a full-fledged deluge started.

Thunder muffled a shot outside the front door. Fargo's eyes flicked up in time to see the lock splinter and disappear. The door swung open.

Angus McCord's huge frame filled the doorway. He gripped a smoking Colt just like Fargo's. Lightning flashed behind Angus, making the sopping-wet mountain man appear even more powerful and dangerous. McCord wore a grizzly-bear coat. Water dripped from his mountaineer's hat with an eagle feather dangling down the back. McCord stepped inside and shut the door. He said, "Fargo, you ready to get out of this jail?"

Fargo came off the bunk grinning. He beat Angus to the bars, stepped away from the cell door, and gestured toward the lock. "Be my guest."

McCord placed five slugs in the locking mechanism. Waving the pungent gunsmoke out of his face, Angus swung the door open and reloaded while Fargo retrieved his weapons. McCord moved over to Fargo and he asked, "Do you want to kill the miserable bastards now or later? They're in the saloon eating with Jack Castle."

"Later. After the mission I'm on."

"Saw the Ovaro standing in the rain. That's how I knew you were here. Went inside the saloon. Clyde Magee was bellied-up to the bar. Remember Magee?"

Nodding, Fargo answered, "You two fought the Apache way back when."

"That's right. Anyhow, after seeing that whore, Melba, and not you, I reckoned the worst. So I pulled Magee aside and asked. He told me you told everybody about the massacre and them Apaches capturing females."

Fargo had to wait for booming thunder to subside, then said, "They headed south with five or more. About twenty riding unshod ponies, and I saw five shod."

"Vásquez," Angus grunted contemptuously.

"Vásquez?" echoed Fargo. "Who's he?"

McCord motioned Fargo to the door, then blew out the lamp. Fargo opened the door. McCord stood looking out over his shoulder when answering, "A mixed-blood. Part Apache, part Mexican, part white. Mean sonsabitch. Meaner than those four breeds that ride with him, but only slightly. Vásquez murdered his mother and father when he was a kid. Cut their heads plumb off and fed them to the dogs. Then he ate the dogs. He's mad. You know, deranged.

"I've been gone for the last six months," Angus explained. "Just now got back. Magee's been looking after the trading post. Had to get out of Beaver Pond. Too much noise. Went to the high country to get a little peace and tranquillity. Magee told me the massacres started right after I left. He told me about Vásquez riding with the Apache."

During McCord's pause, Fargo feared the worst for Annie Hogg. A brilliant bolt of lightning struck a tree across the street. Fargo saw Angus had brought the Ovaro and his saddled dun. Hitched to the rail beside them stood Ott's and Silas' horses.

Angus went on to say, "Vásquez and his boys get Apaches to do most of the killing. He takes the females. That is, he takes those young enough to sell or trade. Vásquez shoots the rest. Guns 'em down in cold blood, or so I hear tell."

"Sell or trade?" Fargo wondered aloud.

"Yeah," Angus replied. "Vásquez sells 'em to miners or prospectors, whoever. He also takes gold and trades for mules, horses, guns, whatever he can get when the taker has no cash."

"How long has this been going on, Angus? The army—"

McCord's snort cut him off. "Army knows about Vásquez, all right. But they can't catch him. Moves around. Been going on for a year now, ever since Jack Castle came to town and bought out Bo Weathers. Castle is a crafty one, all right. Was a tin-horn gambler back in Wichita. A cheater."

Fargo was way ahead of this part in McCord's story. He said, "Castle brought Buck Ott and Silas Ferguson to Beaver Pond, didn't he?"

"How'd you know that?"

"I get around," Fargo answered wryly.

McCord continued, "I think Jack Castle and Vásquez are in cahoots with each other. That meadow is a mighty popular massacre site for Vásquez and his gang. Before I left, I watched Ott and Silas ride south often. Never followed 'em to see where they went. I can put two and two together, though."

"And what does it add up to?"

"Round trip takes 'em exactly half the time for 'em to get to Clearview Hill."

"I know the place. Go on."

"Then you know you can see for miles. They watch for wagon trains. When they see one on the trail, they take off for Vásquez's hideout. Next thing we hear about is Apaches have carried out another massacre at the meadow. That's the distance it takes for a slow-moving wagon train to get there. And fast-riding Apache who know all the shortcuts."

Nodding toward the dun, Fargo asked, "You riding with me?"

"Yeah. I've been waiting for somebody tough as a boot like you to come along. Don't see any trailsmen with your skills anymore. Besides, this place is getting too big and loud for me."

"Disturbs your peace and tranquillity?" Fargo chuckled over his shoulder.

"Dang right," McCord shot back.

Fargo stepped out into the downpour and went straight to the rear of Ott's and Silas' mounts. The second hoof he lifted had a missing shoe.

Getting in his saddle, Angus asked, "What're you looking for?"

Easing up in his, Fargo told him, "Missing shoe. I think I found the horse that threw it."

"Which one?"

Fargo pointed to the horse.

"Silas Ferguson's," McCord said.

They turned and rode south and out of Beaver Pond.

Coming to the meadow, Angus asked, "I know we're heading for New Mexico Territory, but to where, when we get there?"

"To Enchanted Mountain. I want to get with Chief Rain Dances."

Angus McCord halted the dun instantly and howled, "Oh, no, not him. Fargo, Rain Dances is a crafty bastard. What do you want from him?"

"A vision." Fargo chuckled. "The man partakes of peyote. You know that."

"I'm not smoking or drinking that stuff again," McCord complained bitterly. "The one time I did with him, I saw all sorts of crazy things in my brain."

Fargo had heard the story about McCord's experience with peyote. Angus saw himself running naked across the desert, chased by two equally naked Acoma Indian maidens, Chief Rain Dances' daughters. Blue Corn was obese, according to Angus, and her twin was a bag of bones, when, in fact, Blue Corn was fleshy and Doe's Tail shapely. To hear Angus describe his hallucination, Blue Corn's body shook and bounced all over when running after him. Angus said Blue Corn's fat tits were slamming against her face most of the time. Doe's Tail's were shrunken, as were the nipples on her bony chest.

Angus had run until he collapsed from the heat and exhaustion. Blue Corn waited while her sister sucked on Angus' member to get it good and hard. According to Angus, he screamed everytime Doe's Tail bucked teeth raked his organ, which was often. When Doe's Tail finished, Blue Corn squatted over it and sat down hard, her weight all but killing the mountain man, according to him. It got worse. Blue Corn started bouncing on it. Worse still, according to Angus, Doe's Tail sat on his face, nearly choking him to death.

The hallucination effect of the peyote eventually wore off. Angus said he smelled rotten fish, then tasted hair. Opening his eyes, he found himself on a dirt floor of a room in a hovel, his face high between Blue Corn's thighs. When he moved, she awakened and jammed his face back down, according to Angus.

Fargo knew Angus' bawling like he did was out of fear of Blue Corn. So he said, "Look, you don't have to take any peyote. And if it will make you happy, I'll take Blue Corn off your hands."

"What about the other one?" Angus asked warily.

"Doe's Tail, too," Fargo replied.

"You'd do that for me? Take on both of the crazy bitches? You aren't lying, are you, Fargo? Tricking me?"

"Yes, to the first two, no to the other two. Are you coming or not?"

McCord told his dun to "Giddyup."

No more was said about the twins or peyote after that. They continued riding in the rain. Streams of mud flowed down the trail. Slowly the hard rainfall changed to drizzle. The overcast wasn't moisture-laden enough or dense enough to deny the bright morning sun. Fargo watched the darkness of night slowly give way to dawn. Shortly thereafter the drizzle petered out. Then they rode under leaden skies until their heads drooped. Sleepy eyes vaguely saw the puddles or drying runoffs that reached for gulleys carved by previous ones.

Dawn changed to day, daylight to darkness before they halted for the night. While they worked—Angus erecting a lean-to, Fargo making a small fire—they chatted, mostly about the advancing frontier. After eating a trail meal of beef jerky and sharing a tin of beans that McCord had brought along, they slept. Or rather, Angus did. Fargo tried. The big mountain man's loud snores kept the Trailsman awake. No amount of elbow-jabbing McCord's ribs shut him up. Fargo moved his bedroll twenty yards away from the snoring man. He still couldn't sleep for hearing the noise. Fargo moved his bedding another twenty yards, to a spot behind an outcrop. Knowing McCord still snored, he listened for it. He moved a third time, this time fifty yards farther away from the gagging sounds. Only after burying his head inside the bedroll and clamping his hands over his ears did Fargo find relief and go to sleep.

Angus kicking his leg woke him. "Get up, Fargo. Coffee's on."

Fargo groaned as his head poked from the bedroll. Dawn was breaking. The sky was overcast, leaden.

"Thought you'd run away and left me," Angus muttered. "Till I saw your black-and-white. Whatcha doing way over here, anyhow?"

Fargo stared up at him and said evenly, "Angus McCord, I don't want to hear you preach peace and tranquillity ever again." He watched Angus' brow furrow, a puzzled expression form on his face. "Don't show me that look of innocence, Angus. You know what I'm talking about."

Shrugging, Angus replied, "No I don't. You gonna tell me?"

"Snoring, Angus. Loud as hell. It sounded like a billy goat strangling to death. Angus, you snore."

McCord's expression changed to genuine shock as he said, "I do? Sure you weren't having a nightmare?"

Fargo stood and started rolling up his bedroll. "No nightmares, Angus. Your snoring is real. It's no wonder one end of your roof is caving in. Now, let's go see how you make coffee."

Angus mumbled to himself all the way to the fire. Fargo secured the bedroll behind his saddle, then filled a tin cup with the blackest brew he'd ever seen. Angus watched with anticipation as Fargo took a sip. Gagging, he spit it out and said, "Jesus, McCord, are you out to poison me? That stuff would kill a grizzly."

"Did, in fact. A she-grizzly."

Fargo watched him drain his cup, then smack his lips. "A she-grizzly?"

McCord smiled. Fargo knew one of Angus' famous tall tales was forthcoming. Angus began, "She and me were hibernating together, and—"

"I don't want to hear about it," Fargo broke in. "Maybe later. Right now, I'm in a foul mood." Shaking his head, Fargo poured the coffee onto the fire and muttered to himself, "Got no sleep and he gives me runny shit for coffee. Damn."

"What did you say?"

"I said mount up. Time we were leaving."

3

Just before sunset Enchanted Mountain came into view. From their distance they saw it as a barren column that towered up through the low-hanging clouds, its flat top unseen. In fact, the mountain wasn't a mountain at all, but a butte composed of pure rock, evidenced by the many that had fallen all around it and formed its upward-sweeping base. The natural shape of the majestic pillar, its four surfaces, was much larger than it appeared to them from a distance. Up close, the silent sentinel would be humbling.

The Indians who lived in the adobe hovels on a high plateau beyond Enchanted Mountain, and in clear sight of it, considered the mountain as having magical powers; hence its name.

One path, and only one, led up to and down from the plateau, making it easy for the Acoma to defend their stronghold, which accounted for their longevity.

Enchanted Mountain rose up from a wide valley floor, dwarfing the plateaus on either side. The valley was green with undergrowth and grass and cedar trees.

Coming closer to the tower of rock, Fargo saw an Acoma boy taking a small goat herd to the village.

They passed the goats just short of the path leading up to the pueblo. Fargo nodded to the boy, who stared at him.

Angus went up first. Fargo heard him muttering, "Please, Lord, don't let me use any of that peyote while I'm up here. And, please, keep Blue Corn and her sister away from me."

A crowd had gathered at the top of the path to watch the two white men arrive. Both Angus and Fargo spoke enough of the Acoma language to make themselves understood. The Acoma had to speak slowly for them to understand.

Coming to the top, Angus told one Indian, "Brothers, we come in peace and—"

Fargo interrupted before he could add tranquillity. "To sit with Chief Rain Dances."

The crowd parted, then quickly surrounded and led them into the labyrinth of passageways designed long before the Acoma saw a mustang. The adobe hovels lining either side of the tight corridor shared common walls and a single flat roof. Fargo's and McCord's boots scraped adobe as they negotiated their way through the maze. Smoke from cooking fires carried the aroma of roasting *cabrito*.

The part of the crowd in front of Fargo stopped. An Acoma man looked at an opening, an entrance without a door, and said, "Chief Rain Dances."

They dismounted and wedged around the horses to the opening.

Angus said, "Uh, I'll look after our horses." He glanced nervously toward the opening.

A deep voice from within said, "Wait." A short, frail man with a heavily wrinkled face stepped into the entrance.

McCord gulped loudly.

Fargo said, "How, Chief Rain Dances."

The chief looked up at him and in good English said, "Cut the Indian bullshit, Trailsman. Come inside. Both of you." Glancing at McCord, he told him, "Your horses will be fed and watered." Looking back to Fargo, he went on, "A lookout saw you in the valley. He came and told me two white men were approaching, one, tall and riding a big black-and-white horse. I knew at once it was you. Nobody else rides a horse like that." Rain Dances turned and went back inside.

Fargo heard McCord whispering, "Please, Lord, don't let me do it," as he entered.

Fargo recognized the purpose of the room at once. Twice as large as all others, it was used for conducting spiritual ceremonies, of which peyote was an integral part. A small fire burned in the center of an open space.

Ten men sat around the fire, their stolid gazes fixed on the flickering flames, as though already in trances. None so much as batted an eyelid when Rain Dances sat. He motioned Angus to sit on his left, Fargo on his right.

The old chief asked, "Why do you come, Trailsman? Why do you, mountain man?"

Fargo answered. "A few days ago a man named Vásquez—"

"I know of whom you speak," Rain Dances cut in to acknowledge. "Vásquez is a bad man. Continue."

"He and Apaches massacred white people on a wagon train north of here. They stole the women and took them south. I was hoping you would be able to tell Angus and me where they are." Fargo looked at the small clay bowls used for drinking peyote and the pipes for smoking it held by several of the men.

Rain Dances nodded, grunted. "I will help you."

Fargo noticed McCord's eyes were riveted on the bowls as the peyote ceremony got under way. Soon sweat appeared on McCord's brow, collected, and trickled down his nose. Fargo knew his friend was having visions of waking up with his face in Blue Corn's crotch.

The muddy-appearing peyote mixture was poured from a large clay pot into the smaller bowls. Rain Dances started them around the circle. Pipes were put to lips and lit. Soon the space was filled with smoke carrying the unmistakable odor of peyote. Rain Dances sipped from his bowl and gestured for his guests to do the same.

Fargo touched tightly closed lips to the rim of his bowl, over which he watched Angus McCord. The mountain man had the bowl in a death grip with both hands, staring at the thick liquid as though it were a deadly rattler poised to strike. Slowly, reluctantly at first, Angus took a sip, then two fast swallows, after which his shoulders sagged and he emitted a sigh.

An hour later all but Fargo were in the grip of the hallucinative, rocking back and forth slowly, chanting lowly, with their eyes closed.

Fargo moved quietly behind Angus, took him under the arms, and slowly, softly, dragged him outside. Dropping the huge man against the outer surface next to the entranceway, he asked a passerby directions to Chief Rain Dances' living quarters. The man told him he would take him. Fargo carried McCord's deadweight on his back through the maze to an opening like all the others, where his guide stopped and called Blue Corn out.

She broke into a wide smile upon seeing Angus. Motioning Fargo to enter, she stepped aside for him to pass.

Doe's Tail sat by the fire, gnawing roasted meat off a goat's rib. Her eyes followed Fargo's movements as he dumped Angus onto a blanket along one wall. Angus' eyes were wide open and glazed, of course. He neither saw nor heard anything; neither did he snore. Fargo reckoned Angus was too busy running to snore.

Blue Corn sat and put Angus' hand in her lap and began rocking gently.

Doe's Tail offered Fargo a handful of ribs, which he gladly accepted. He sat across the fire from her. She watched him eat while stripping the rib clean. She tossed the bone outside for the dogs to gnaw on, sucked the juice from her fingers, and said matter-of-factly, "I'll sleep with you tonight. Blue Corn gets him."

Fargo looked at the shapely young woman. Painted by the dancing shadows of the flames, the petite girl's unblemished skin glistened, her face conveying the mystique of most Indians. Fargo nodded.

Doe's Tail stood facing him and provocatively pulled her dress over her head and dropped it on the hard-packed earth floor. Their eyes met and locked as she fondled her firm but small breasts. Tweaking the large nipples, she asked, "Are you ready for me, Trailsman?"

He glanced at Blue Corn, who was taking off Angus' clothes, oblivious to anyone else in the room.

"Put your dress back on," he said, rising. "Take me to my horse."

She gasped, "Your horse?"

"Yes, I have to get something."

Doe's Tail wiggled the dress down her body, then crooked a finger for him to come on. She held his hand as she hurried him along to the goat pen. The Ovaro knickered when he saw Fargo. He stepped over the top rail of the pen and saw they had unsaddled the horses and piled everything in a corner of the shed. He fetched his bedroll.

The Ovaro was right behind him, nudging with his head. Fargo paused to scratch the stallion's face. Looking into his big black eyes, Fargo murmured, "I know, boy. Goats stink like hell." The stallion knickered lowly, as though he understood.

Doe's Tail, leaning on the rail fence, said, "You going to sleep with me on that horse?" Her tone of voice was laced with impatience.

"I'm coming," Fargo answered.

They weaved their way back to Rain Dances' hovel. She started to enter. He pulled her back. She spun in time to glimpse his bedroll go over the edge of the roof. Fargo boosted her up on it, then pressed over the edge. Doe's Tail already had the bedroll spread out and was shucking her dress.

She reclined and fondled her small, firm breasts while watching Fargo start to pull off his boots and shirt.

Fargo watched the trailing edge of the low-hanging cloud deck pass overhead swiftly, leaving a star-filled sky. He removed his gun belt and laid it on the roof, then released the belt buckle and pulled down his Levi's.

Doe's Tail couldn't wait. She sat and pulled his underdrawers down to his knees. In that instant the clouds passed over Enchanted Mountain and left it gleaming in the bright moonlight, glistening from moisture. Looking at the butte, Fargo heard her say, "It's so big and hard," and he didn't know whether she referred to his organ or the mighty butte. He felt her small hands coil around his member and looked down in time to see her put it in her mouth.

He listened to her sucking, enjoying herself for a while, then entwined his fingers in her raven, short hair and gently pulled her head back.

She clung to his member and said, "I want more of it. Please?"

He stepped out of the Levi's and underdrawers, saying,

"And you will . . . all of it." Fargo pushed the tiny young woman to lie on his bedding, then straddled her chest and eased down until his hard butt met her stiff nipples.

She raised her head, put the crown in her mouth, and swished her hot tongue around it several times before taking in more. Her hands gripped his buttock cheeks and pulled him to her, forcing more of his member deep inside her hot mouth. He listened to her moans of happiness a moment or two longer before rocking back to withdraw.

"You taste good, Trailsman," she mewed. "Why did you make me stop?"

He lay beside her and rolled her onto his muscular body and said, "I'd suffocate you, Doe's Tail, under me. I'd crush you." He spread her legs and bent the knees for her to straddle him at the waist.

She leaned forward and grazed his lips teasingly with her nipples. He caught one and sucked the entire mound into his mouth. As he circled her nipple with his tongue, she squealed her delight. He shifted to the other breast and began sucking it.

Doe's Tail's head lolled as she moaned, "Take me, Trailsman . . . take me now!"

He moved his hands down to her tense buttock cheeks and stopped sucking on the breast. She sat up, raised on her knees, and pulled his throbbing member that had lodged in her crack into position. Raising her hips higher, she put the head between her hot, moist lips and squatted, forcing it in, and gasped, "Oh . . . oh, my . . . so big . . . so nice."

He pushed gently, entering her velvety sheath partway. She groaned as she pushed down to capture all of him. Fargo started a slow up-and-down rhythm, which she quickly met. Doe's Tail's fingers clawed and dug into his pectoral muscles as she tilted her head back and moaned rapturously, "Faster, Trailsman . . . go faster."

He pumped, she gyrated, gasping, "Oh, oh—that's it . . . that's it," and screamed skyward, "Aaagh . . . aaayeeeii!"

Fargo was amazed that the tiny package could take his

full length, but she did, welding her parted lips to his base and rubbing it high on the top of her opening to maximize the pleasure. As she did, her breathing noticeably quickened. She gulped as he felt her first spasm signaling her first orgasm. There were three more and she moaned joyously throughout them. "Deeper, Trailsman . . . go deeper. Push harder, too. Oh, oh . . . yes, yes, yes."

He felt a mighty contraction seize his throbbing member, which was in as far as it would go, then start milking. She gasped when he erupted, "Aaah . . . so hot . . . I am on fire. Flood me, Trailsman, with your lava."

Doe's Tail reached behind her butt. Fargo felt her hands massaging his tight scrotum. Finally, she fell forward, gasping for breath, and bit his chest.

Fargo nestled her head in the crook of his shoulder. Rubbing her little Acoma ass, he said, "You were good, Doe's Tail. Better than most."

"Better than my sister?" she murmured.

She referred to the last time he was in Acoma village. The twins were almost thirteen or fourteen, maybe sixteen—they didn't know their age—and being petite and not yet filled out, it was only natural for Fargo to assume they were innocent young girls. He took Blue Corn for a ride in the valley. She threw herself at him. He had to pull her off. Apparently she subsequently told Doe's Tail she'd lain with him.

"I wouldn't know," he said. "Go to sleep."

She circled an arm around his neck, drew his face to hers, and they kissed hotly, passionately, openmouthed.

At dawn, somebody making a hell of a racket snapped Fargo's eyes open. His gun hand automatically went to his Colt as he listened, now wide awake and keenly alert. He pushed Doe's Tail off him, rolled over to the edge of the roof, and peered down.

Angus stood looking down. His bare feet were spread wide and his arms extended forward with his hands planted against the adobe wall. The naked mountain man was vomiting loudly.

Fargo uncocked the Colt and said, " 'Morning, Angus. Rough night? That puke smells like spoiled fish."

Angus spit a stream. Without looking up, he muttered sickly, "You big bastard, I'm gonna beat you within an inch of your life for lying to me." He paused, hawked spit, before adding, "No I ain't. I'm gonna shove your face 'tween her stinking fat thighs and hold it there while I listen to you gag and choke." He heaved again.

Fargo said, "It's the peyote, Angus. You overdid it, is all. It leaves an awful aftertaste in your mouth. That's what's making you puke your guts out. Up beside peyote, pussy tastes sweet."

"Then I'm gonna beat your brains out."

Fargo watched him drag the back of his hand across his mouth, step back, and look up. Fargo shot him a wink and a grin, saying, "Get dressed. I'll come down and we'll talk to the chief. He is in there?"

Angus shook his head. "He never came home. Shit, I feel terrible. Sick as hell."

"It'll pass. Pull on your clothes. I'll do the same and come down. Meet you outside."

As Angus staggered through the opening, Fargo heard him mumble, "Aftertaste, shit. It was her."

Fargo awakened Doe's Tail and told her to take his bedroll back to the goat pen, that he was going to see her father.

Rubbing sleep from her eyes, she said, "I want more of you, Trailsman. A lot more. The next time, lie on me. I want to feel your big muscles against my body."

Dressing, he said, "I don't know when the next time will be. Right after talking with your father, we'll be heading out."

He bent and kissed her on the lips. She curled both arms around his neck and tried to pull him down with her. Peeling her arms away, he reminded her not to forget the bedroll.

Fargo hung over the side and dropped to the ground. " 'Bout ready, Angus? Or are you eating fish again?"

McCord charged through the opening, tackling Fargo around the waist. They rolled on the ground, pounding each other momentarily, then both burst out laughing.

Lying there, McCord admitted, "You know, it was peyote aftertaste, just like you said." Angus got to his feet and pulled Fargo up.

At the ceremonial space, they found Chief Rain Dances sitting with his skinny legs apart and his back against a wall, snoring softly. Fargo coughed discreetly to wake him.

Rain Dances' eyes fluttered open. In a feeble voice and without moving, he said, "This stuff is killing me." Smacking his lips, he added, "The inside of my mouth tastes like shit."

Fargo and McCord squatted. Fargo asked, "Where is Vásquez? The spirits did show you the place?"

Rain Dances leaned forward, rubbed his face, and said, "In Diablo Canyon."

Fargo glanced at McCord and raised his eyebrows.

McCord said, "I know where it is. Between here and Colorado."

The old chief had more to say. "Six females are with him. Two are young girls. They are crying."

"Thanks," Fargo said. "I owe you for this information. What would you like to have?"

"Oh, I don't know. Ponies for my girls would be nice."

"I'll send them by Angus here, next time he comes to Acoma."

"Who said I'd be coming back?" Angus grunted.

Rising, Fargo answered smugly, "You will, now that you know it was the peyote." Looking down at Rain Dances, Fargo said, "Take care, my friend."

Fargo and Angus left the old man sitting there, rubbing his face. They went to the goat pen and made their horses ready for the trail. Fargo noticed Doe's Tail hadn't done what he asked.

McCord volunteered, "She probably went back to sleep."

They stopped at the hovel. Fargo stood in the stirrups and looked on the roof. As McCord had said, she was buried inside his bedroll. He whistled. The Ovaro perked his ears. Doe's Tail's head appeared. Fargo said, "Hand me that bedroll."

She dropped it down to him, saying, "I wanted to remember your smell."

McCord chuckled while watching Fargo tie down his bedroll.

The Trailsman looked up at her as he touched the brim of his hat. Nudging the stallion to walk, he told her, "See you next time. We will go riding in the valley."

Angus McCord guffawed.

4

The Trailsman and the mountain man rode past Enchanted Mountain and out of the valley. Turning north, they headed for Diablo Canyon, a day's ride away. Both men watched the sky. At first puffy clouds appeared in the west. That was about high noon. By midafternoon, thunderclouds had built in the distance.

Rain showers soon slanted down from three of the towering clouds. But the rain was yet too far away for them to be concerned. In the late afternoon, enough ground heat had risen to trigger lightning in the dark clouds, which were collecting and expanding. As they entered Diablo Canyon, all hell broke loose.

A fierce, cold wind greeted the two riders. The wind whipped and lashed, set the trees to oscillating, bending, snapping the trunks of several as if they were twigs. Lightning bolts stabbed down from the churning bottoms of the massive, black clouds, struck trees, and exploded. One struck a large cedar less than ten yards in front of the dun. It exploded in a blinding flash—the immediate area instantly turned garish bright—and peeled the bark from the cedar. The sharp *caarackk* that accompanied the brilliant flash was deafening. The dun and pinto knickered nervously and shook their heads. For a moment they breathed ozone left by the mighty blast.

Thunder boomed, jarring the two men, then rumbled in the canyon and reverberated off its walls. Another, more mighty than the first, presented a spectacular pyrotechnical display that rent the boiling clouds, ripping them as giant hands tearing a thick sheet of canvas.

Then the downpour came in Diablo Canyon.

Whipped by the unrelenting wind, the big, icy raindrops hit and stung them like bullets. Streams instantly manifested where none had been a few seconds ago. Fargo and McCord were forced to take higher ground.

McCord pointed to an overhanging ledge and shouted above the screaming wind and rain, "It's the driest, wettest place around. You want to stop and use it?"

Shaking his head, Fargo answered, "No. I intend to finish what we are here to do. Those shitheads have lived long enough."

Angus nodded grimly and snuggled his bearskin coat tighter.

"How long is this canyon, anyhow?" Fargo yelled.

"Long," Angus shouted back. "We'll reach the end 'bout two miles farther."

"End? Is it boxed? You didn't mention that."

"Yes, it's boxed."

Now Fargo knew he wanted to proceed. Vásquez and his gang would be completely trapped.

Fargo and Angus picked their way among rocks and cedars for another mile or so. The Trailsman's keen sense of smell detected a trace of smoke in the wind and rain. He halted and shouted, "Smoke! We're in luck. They're on this side. Close. Damn close."

"Yes, now I smell it too. I bet they are pinned right against the back wall."

"Any way out?"

"Not that I know of. The wall is sheer and solid rock. Escape is impossible in this storm."

Fargo double-checked that his Colt and Sharps were fully loaded. He returned the Sharps to its saddle case and waved McCord forward. Angus came abreast of him. Fargo told him his plan, "Can't see it, but in this weather we will probably ride right to the front door before we do. When we get there, you back up a short distance. Keep the door in sight. I'll go high and flush them out for you. You know what to do."

McCord nodded.

They began a slow approach.

The smoke became more pronounced.

Lightning flashed.

They halted.

Before them, about ten feet away, stood a hastily built four-sided structure having a flat roof. The saplings Vásquez's men had used had many gaps between them. Firelight spilled through the gaps. Fargo made out the forms of four horses in among a stand of aspens on the downside of the flimsy structure. Maybe there will be the fifth, he hoped. He saw a ledge just above the left side of the cabin. Deerskins hung down from what was obviously the opening to the hideout.

A girlish, sobbing voice begged, "Stop! Please stop. You're hurting me. Please stop!"

Fargo leaned over and cupped a hand to McCord's left ear. "Change in plan. I'll climb up on that ledge, jump, and crash through the roof. I'll shoot as many of the surprised bastards as I can. You get the rest."

McCord nodded.

Fargo dismounted.

Watching him get into position, Angus drew his Colt and thumbed the hammer back.

Fargo jumped high and came down on the roof feet-first. Angus watched him shatter the roof and disappear through the debris.

Fargo landed on his feet, Colt in hand, and instantly blew a hunk of skull and brains out of the half-breed's head who had one of the girls on hands and knees, screwing her.

The other breeds went for their guns.

Fargo swung his Colt and fired point-blank into the heart of one. Continuing to swing, he shot another in the shoulder, knocking him backward. The fourth man fled through the opening. Fargo heard McCord's Colt bark once.

It was over in the blink of an eye. The stunned females were so surprised they didn't even scream. Fargo looked at the naked females and said, "We've come to free you all." To the youngest girl he asked, "Honey, you okay?"

Drawing up her knees to hide her small breasts, she nodded.

Angus parted the deerskins and stepped inside just as the half-breed with the shoulder wound groaned. Fargo went and pulled him into a sitting position and growled, "Are you Vásquez?"

"No hablo inglés," the man groaned, shaking his head.

Shifting to Spanish, Fargo asked, "What does that head shake mean? Speak up, or I'll finish you off here and now."

The badly bleeding man—Fargo knew that he would bleed to death—replied, *"No comprendo."*

At the same time, two of the women said, "Vásquez is gone." One of them added, "He left earlier this morning."

After searching the wounded man for a hideout or knife, Fargo asked him, "Where did Vásquez go?"

He answered, *"No comprendo."*

Fargo pulled him to his feet and shoved the man outside.

"Why didn't you kill him?" one of the girls gasped.

McCord answered wryly, "Ma'am, he won't get far in this weather before he dies. Bullets are expensive."

Fargo glanced around to find their clothes. Seeing none, he presumed Vásquez had taken the precaution of destroying all clothing to help prevent their escaping. "Might as well stay here for the night," he suggested to Angus.

Angus put two logs on the fire.

The women moved into a corner, where they huddled and watched the two men.

Fargo went outside and got his and McCord's bedrolls. Returning, he tossed the bedding to the women and asked, "Which one of you is Annie Hogg?"

"I'm Annie Hogg," a shapely, young blonde answered. "How did you know my name?"

"Your father told me."

A shocked expression crossed her face as she asked, "He's alive?"

"No, he died." Fargo scanned the others' faces and added, "They are all dead. I buried them. All, that is, but one other survivor, who I suspect was a man. Did any of you see him get away? Please tell us your names."

"I'm Helga Emerson," a slim redhead said. She patted a shoulder of the girl who was being raped when Fargo came through the roof. "And this is my daughter, Henrietta."

Fargo glanced to the other girl. The fleshy brunette holding her close said, "She's Martha Enlow. Apaches killed her ma. My name's Eva Stohl."

Another brunette, shorter than the first, volunteered, "I'm Inez Tucker. I know they killed my husband, Hector."

A sandy-haired young woman—Fargo guessed she was no older than twenty-one—with broad hips said, "Name's Ruth Adcock. I saw Ma and Pa get shot by the Apaches."

Helga volunteered in a hollow voice, "No. Vásquez had his men take us into the woods. We were out of sight of what was happening to the others. God, it was awful. It happened so fast." She looked at the two girls. "They killed little Martha's mother. She's only thirteen." Shifting her gaze to her daughter, she continued, "Henrietta's twelve." The woman paused, then blurted, "The beasts! You should have killed him. I had to watch what they did to my baby." Mother and daughter held each other even tighter and started sobbing, rocking back and forth.

It went without saying that Vásquez and the half-breeds had also raped the other five females.

Fargo moved to one front corner, Angus to the other. They watched the rain pour through the section of the roof Fargo had destroyed. The water soon covered the earth floor. All of them watched the water putting out the fire while listening to it spit and sizzle. The space became pitch-black. When lightning flashed, Fargo saw Annie staring at him grim-jawed. He repositioned his spine on the timbers, pulled his hat down over his eyes, and drifted to sleep, wondering where Vásquez had gone and whether or not he'd ever face the man. He hoped he would.

Dawn broke over Diablo Canyon. A light drizzle fell. Fargo's eyes opened slowly to see Angus and the women wide awake, watching him. McCord said, " 'Morning, Fargo. We reckoned you needed the sleep."

Yawning, Fargo stretched kinks out of his muscled body, saying, "Let's get out of here. We have a long ride." He stood and pushed the deerskins back and looked outside.

McCord took off his bearskin coat and pitched it to the women. "One of you can cover yourself with it."

Fargo ripped the deerskins from the opening and tossed them to the girls. "Wrap them around you." Pulling off his shirt, he pitched it to Annie.

McCord said, "If you ladies will turn your heads . . ." When they quickly obeyed, he stripped and took off his long johns. Pulling his pants back on, he told them they could look. He handed Helga his long johns, Inez Tucker his buckskin shirt. Fargo pulled off his Levi's and gave them to Eva.

Fargo told them to bring the bedding. He and Angus went outside to their horses. Stroking his stallion's powerful neck, he said to Angus, "I'll ride ahead and watch for Vásquez. I want him real bad."

McCord nodded. He looked at the three horses tethered to aspens.

Fargo said, "Like you said, the one I wounded won't get far. They'll have to ride double till we find his horse."

The women filed out of the opening. Annie handed Fargo his bedroll and said, "We were to meet my cousin, Tessa, in Wagon Wheel Gap. How am I to get there?"

"I'll take you. I promised your father I would look after you." He tied his bedroll behind his saddle. Easing up into it, he added, "After we buy new clothes for you, we ride for the Gap." He touched the brim of his hat and set the Ovaro to walk.

He found the man he'd shot facedown in mud less than a mile away. Dead, of course. His horse stood nearby. Fargo dismounted, stripped the dead man of clothing, and muttered, "You don't need these rags anymore." He dropped the clothes over the fellow's saddle and tethered the horse to a cedar.

Mounting up, Fargo continued on his way.

When he came to the beginning of Diablo Canyon, he took to higher ground to wait for the others while he watched for Vásquez. Fifteen minutes passed, then thirty, before he saw Angus leading them single-file through the cedars and around larger rocks.

A shot split the air.

The slug whizzed by Fargo's head, close enough to disturb his hair.

He came off the saddle, withdrawing the Sharps from its saddle case during the swift movement.

Another shot rang out. Then another, followed by a third.

Fargo saw all three hit under Annie's mount.
McCord shouted, "Above you! To your right!"
Fargo dived behind a boulder. Peering around one end, he spotted a rifle barrel aimed at him from a crack between two outcrops of rock on top of the canyon wall. He raised the Sharps and emptied it on the crack. Pulling back to reload, he yelled to McCord, "Do you see him?"
"No," Angus called back.
Fargo peered around the boulder again and saw the rifle barrel hadn't moved. He suspected the man had darted behind another boulder.
A revolver barked.
The bullet kissed off the boulder and whined harmlessly into the drizzling rain.
"He's still there," McCord shouted. "Farther to the right."
Another shot was fired at Annie, and missed. Fargo saw the wisp of smoke coming out of the revolver barrel, and the brawny, bronze-skinned man holding it. Fargo lay down a blistering fire at the scant target.
While Fargo was reloading, the man yelled, "We will meet again, *amigo*. You took what was mine. Next time you won't be so lucky. *Adiós*."
Fargo heard hoofbeats pounding on shale atop the ridge.
McCord shouted, "He's gone."
Rising cautiously from his crouch, Fargo saw the rifle had also disappeared. He rode down to join McCord and the women.
Annie said, "That was Vásquez."
"Figured as much," Fargo replied. Eva handed back his Levi's. She now wore the dead man's. Martha wore his shirt.
"Why didn't you kill the bastard?" Helga lamented.
"Tried to, ma'am," Fargo answered. Turning to Angus, he said, "I'll go track him. If I don't catch up to him, I'll meet you at Clearview Hill."
Angus nodded.
Fargo tipped his hat, saying, "Ladies," then rode away at a gallop.
Atop the ridge he picked up Vásquez's tracks easily

enough. They headed northwest. He followed them for about an hour before losing them in dense undergrowth that covered rocky terrain as far as he could see. Giving up the hunt, he turned toward Clearview Hill.

Shortly, the drizzle ceased. The clouds passed overhead and left a warm sun hanging in the pretty blue sky. Fargo's spirits picked up immediately with the sun's appearance, and he rode with renewed vigor.

Angus and the females were waiting for him on the trail at the base of the hill.

Fargo shook his head.

Angus said, "Don't feel bad. That's some of the roughest country in the territory." Glancing over his powerfully built shoulder, he said, "All right, ladies, mount up and we'll be on our way."

As Annie stretched up into the saddle, the tail on Fargo's shirt she wore hiked up. He glimpsed what appeared to be a tattoo on the left cheek of her shapely fanny. Blinking, he decided he was wrong, that he'd probably just seen specks of mud on the cheek.

Coming to the small meadow, he knew they would want to see where he had buried their loved ones. They halted, got off their horses, and gathered around the grave.

When they started wailing and wringing their hands and lying on the common grave, the emotion was too much for the men. They walked to the knoll to wait for the females to vent their feelings.

Listening to the girls crying, McCord said, "Fargo, I knew there was a reason I stuck with you as long as I have."

"Oh, what's that, Angus?" Fargo muttered.

Nodding toward the grave site, Angus answered, "That. Frankly, I didn't think we'd find them, much less alive. I had planned on leaving you at Acoma. *Before* we went up to the village, of course."

"Why didn't you?"

Angus answered obliquely. "Fact is, I like Beaver Pond. Best years of my life till Castle arrived. I don't know how many times I was ready to chuck it all after he bought out Bo. Hell, Bo and me got along. Once I went so far as saddling my horse. Then you came along and gave me a reason to stay. Hell, you were a crutch."

Fargo wanted to hear him tell the real reason, because Angus himself needed to know it. Only then would Angus get it out of his system. Fargo pressed, "Angus, I ask again, why didn't you leave me when we got to Acoma?"

Angus scratched his head and looked away.

Fargo knew his huge friend was wrestling with his conscience.

Finally, the mountain man admitted, "I, uh, I . . . Dammit, they aren't gonna run me out of my own town. That's why I stuck. I'm going back to Beaver Pond and clean 'em out, make the place decent again, get back my peace and tranquillity."

"Good," Fargo replied. "And I'll help you do just that."

They went back to the women and told them to saddle up, it would be dark soon and they needed to reach Beaver Pond before that.

Again, Fargo glimpsed the mud specks on Annie's rump when she hiked her right leg over the saddle. This time he commented, "Doesn't that mud on your hiney bother you?"

Frowning, Annie looked at him and asked, "What mud? And, Mr. Fargo, I'd appreciate it if you would quit looking at my behind." She slapped the reins on the horse's rump.

They rode into Beaver Pond just as the sun hovered over the mountains west of the little town. A man stepped out of the saloon and saw the two bare-chested men leading the procession. He darted back inside. The saloon promptly emptied to come see. Fargo led the females to the hotel. Easing off the saddle, he told them to wait while he made arrangements.

Inside, the clerk told him the hotel had no vacancies.

Fargo yanked him halfway over the counter and snarled, "I said I want four rooms. Now, you can either ask them to leave, or I'll throw them out. Which is it?"

The fellow's eyes rolled back, and he fainted.

Fargo went behind the counter and got four room keys off the board, then strode to the rooms and let himself in. Three were vacant. The man in the fourth wanted to argue. Fargo put a silver dollar in the angry man's hand and closed his fingers around it with such force that the man groaned. The fellow gathered up his stuff and left.

Fargo went to the hotel's front door and waved everybody inside. Handing them room keys, he said, "Go inside and take our clothes off, then hand them out to us. Lock your doors. You'll be safe. Tomorrow, you will all get new clothes."

The two men waited in the hall. The women started handing out their garments.

Putting on his shirt, McCord said, "This is my fight, Fargo. I allowed them in. Now, I'm going to make 'em pay a penalty."

Nodding, Fargo said, "I'll protect your backside."

They went to the saloon and paused at the double doors to look inside. There were seven patrons, five at the bar, two sitting at a table with Jack Castle, their backs to the swinging doors. Weasel Face stood behind the bar, Melba was on the other side.

Everybody looked at them, including Ray and John Barrow, who were sitting at the table with Castle. McCord walked straight to Castle's table and said, "You and I are gonna play five-card draw. First one to lose a hundred dollars gets killed." He jerked a chair back, put money on the table, and sat.

Castle said, "Angus, I don't want your money and I don't want to kill you. So, why don't you get up and leave?"

"Shuffle those cards," McCord growled.

The men at the bar moseyed over to watch.

McCord won the first pot—ten dollars—with two pair, sevens over fours.

On the next deal, Fargo watched him squeeze a pair of tens, a king, the third seven, and the ace of hearts.

McCord shoved ten dollars out and opened.

Castle covered.

McCord drew three cards and didn't improve the pair of tens. He bet ten dollars.

Castle drew one and folded.

Four more hands were played. On the fifth deal Fargo watched Angus catch three queens, a six, and a deuce.

Castle opened and bet ten dollars.

McCord covered and raised twenty.

Castle hesitated before saying, "Angus, I think you're bluffing."

Expressionless, Angus just stared at him.

Castle slid twenty dollars in the pot.

McCord discarded the deuce. Castle dealt him another six.

Castle took three cards.

McCord looked over the full house at him and said evenly, "Why don't we end this here and now."

Fargo noticed Angus hadn't made his remark a question. He reached down and surreptitiously withdrew his Arkansas toothpick.

Castle answered by moving all of his money to the center of the table.

McCord did the same and showed the full house.

Castle's left hand was palm-down on the table. He spread three kings and the other pair of sixes.

The spectators moved back.

Fargo grabbed the back of Castle's left hand and slowly turned it palm-up to reveal a red eight.

"You cheating bastard," McCord snarled. "I'm gonna hang your sorry ass."

Jack Castle fell backward, toppling his chair. He scrambled to his feet, brandishing a Smith & Wesson.

Fargo drew his Colt and shot the six-gun out of Castle's hand.

Castle ran for the back door.

Melba stuck her foot out and tripped him.

McCord pulled him to his feet and muscled him out the swinging doors. The small crowd followed McCord dragging Castle to the rope Weasel Face had thrown over the sturdy oak limb.

"Somebody get a horse," McCord said, "while I put the noose around this cheater's neck."

Jack Castle started screaming, "Ott! Help me, Ott!"

Snugging the noose tight, McCord grunted, "Shut up. There's nobody to help you."

Fargo saw them first. The four men were spread across the street, walking slowly toward the hanging tree. Weasel Face on the left, Buck Ott next to him and Silas Ferguson, and Vásquez on the right.

Fargo focused on Vásquez's gun hand.

The four halted about ten yards away. McCord stepped out in the dirty street and faced them. Fargo stayed where he was, on the fringe of the crowd. Those gathered to watch the hanging moved back quickly, out of the lines of fire. As they did, Jack Castle jerked the rope from the limb with the noose still around his neck. He ran toward Ott, yelling, "Shoot the sonsabitches. Kill them."

It happened fast.

Six revolvers came out of six holsters.

The mountain man was half a blink faster drawing and firing his than Buck Ott.

Ott catapulted backward, the hole in his heart gushing blood.

Swinging onto Silas, the deputy fired at McCord.

The bullet hit McCord's left upper arm. He fired.

Silas crumbled awkwardly, a hole between his eyes.

Unnerved, Weasel Face jerked his trigger. The two slugs kicked up dust at McCord's feet.

McCord shot him in the gut.

Fargo and Vásquez exchanged shots.

Vásquez's grazed Fargo's shirt sleeve and thudded into the trunk of the oak behind him.

Fargo watched Vásquez be knocked halfway around by the Colt's hot bullet that tore off the right side of his skull.

Jack Castle dropped to his knees. Wringing his hands, he pleaded with McCord, "No! Don't kill me. I'll give you the saloon. I'll leave town and never come back. I promise."

McCord calmly drilled him between the eyes.

It was sundown at Beaver Pond, and all was quiet.

Then female screams erupted within the hotel and shattered the brief peace and tranquillity.

5

Fargo raced to the hotel. Bursting through the front door, he saw the clerk's body draped over the registration counter, his blood dripping into a pool of it. The man's throat had been sliced open.

Gun in hand, Fargo twisted around the corner of the hallway. Lamplight spilled through three doorways to the women's rooms. The door at the end of the hallway was wide open.

He ran to it and heard hooves pounding away, fleeing in the heavy shadows that concealed blue spruce in back of the hotel.

Returning, he looked in on the women and asked Inez, "You people all right? What happened?"

"Two men kicked the door in," she explained. "They came in and looked around, then left. I heard them batter down another door. Will it never end?"

Fargo found the fourth door intact and locked. Banging on it, he shouted, "Are you all right, ma'am?"

He heard a key insert into the locking mechanism and the tumblers fall as it twisted. He watched the doorknob turn slowly and the door be opened by an inch. One of Annie Hogg's brown eyes looked out at him. She was calm when answering, "Yes, Mr. Fargo, I'm all right. What were they looking for?"

"You," he answered dryly.

"What in the world for?" she asked.

"Beats hell out of me—"

"Mr. Fargo, please watch your language," she interrupted coolly.

"Pull a sheet around you. I'm coming in."

"No, you're not. You're staying—"

He shoved the door open and barked, "Now, you tell me what's going on."

Annie backed to the bed, one arm folded across her bosom and a hand covering her crotch. She had to remove one to get it. The arm shielding her bosom darted to the sheet.

Fargo sighed sardonically, "Ma'am, I've already seen you buck-naked."

She whipped the sheet around her body, saying, "That was a different circumstance. What do you want?"

"Answers," he began. "Two men broke into three rooms and all they found were naked females. Then they left. That leads me to believe they were looking for you. Why?"

She sat on the edge of the bed. Frowning, she replied, "I don't know why. Like you, I'm also puzzled."

He moved to stand at the window. Parting the curtains, he looked out, deep in thought. He kept asking himself why they wanted Annie Hogg. What made her so different from the others? There was no apparent problem before the massacre and her capture. Vásquez. The two men. Vásquez had implied he would try to get all the females back. They obviously wanted only Annie. Why was she so important? the Trailsman wondered. His hand dipped into the left front pocket in his Levi's and fingered the pouch of nuggets.

Still staring out the window, he said, "Your father told me you would pay me handsomely if I took you someplace. He died before saying where. Does it have anything to do with this?" He turned and pitched the pouch onto the bed.

She recognized it instantly. Grabbing the pouch, she gasped, "You stole this off my father's body."

"No, I didn't. He gave it to me. What's the story?"

First she dumped the nuggets on the bed and counted them. Putting them back in the pouch, she said, "Good. They're all there." Glaring at him, she continued, "You promised to take me to Wagon Wheel Gap to meet my cousin."

"And so I will, young lady. I keep my promises. I

promised your father I would find you, and I did. I shot and killed four men, including Vásquez in the—"

"Vásquez is dead?" she gasped.

"Stone-cold dead," he muttered.

"When? Where?"

"Out in the street a few minutes ago."

He watched her apparently think a moment before she said, "I'll have to talk to Tessa about this." She glanced at the pouch and went on, saying, "If we were . . ."

Annie Hogg was taxing his patience. He strode toward the door. Passing the bed, he snatched the pouch from her hand. She sucked in a breath. Going through the doorway, he told her, "You get clothes tomorrow." In the hallway he added, "Then we're leaving."

Crossing the lobby, he saw the clerk's body had been taken away and the pool of blood wiped up.

Outside, he led his pinto to the livery. The smithy, a muscular man with flaming red hair, unruly beard and mustache, met him at the entrance. A lantern stood on the ground next to his feet. "Clyde Magee's the name." Clyde wiped his hand before extending it to Fargo.

Shaking it, Fargo said, "McCord mentioned you, but didn't say you were the smithy. Name's Skye Fargo."

"Mighty fine pinto you have there." Magee fingered his beard, glanced at Fargo, and added, "Wouldn't want to sell or trade him, would you?"

"Not for sale or trade."

"Didn't think so. Come on in. I got one empty stall."

Magee carried the lantern to the stall and watched Fargo remove the saddle and other gear before leading the stallion into it.

Fargo told the smithy, "Check his hooves for condition and all shoes for security. Give him good oats and all the hay he wants. I'll come for him about noon tomorrow. Maybe a mite earlier. When I do, I want to buy a good horse and saddle, everything."

"Uh, huh. That'll be Jack Castle's horse and tack. He won't be needing them anymore. I'll have everything ready."

Fargo draped his saddlebags over his shoulder and left. Outside, he noticed the five corpses still lay where they had fallen. Glancing toward the saloon, he decided everybody was too busy celebrating to bother with the dead. He started to go join them, but somebody groaning stopped him. Sure that it came from one of the five men sprawled in the street, he looked at them and frowned. He heard the groan again and saw Weasel Face's body twitch.

Fargo went and squatted next to him. Weasel Face was clutching his gut. He was still alive, all right, but only barely.

Fargo said, "Weasel Face, you know you're dying. Want to say anything before you do? Make an admission? Confession?"

Spitting out a glob of blood, the man groaned so low that Fargo had to lean in to hear the words. "Did they kill her?"

"They, who?" Fargo asked. "Her, who?"

"Hogg."

The bartender was fading fast. Fargo barely heard the word. He bent down and lied, "Yes, they killed her. And got away. Who did it?"

"Good," was the last word uttered by the bartender. His dead hands relaxed and slipped from his bloody abdomen.

Fargo closed the corpse's eyes and then stood and looked at the small hotel. Tugging an earlobe, he muttered, "Thanks, Weasel Face, you confirmed what I suspected." Looking at the saloon, he started walking toward it, telling himself he would soon know the two men's names.

He paused before pushing through the double doors and scanned the room. Only four familiar faces were missing: Castle's, Weasel Face's, and Ray and John Barrow's. Angus McCord was the center of attention. He stood at the middle of the bar, flanked by the others. Sad-eyed Melba was behind the bar, serving liquor like there would be no tomorrow.

Fargo pushed his way inside and wedged between McCord and a man. He saw McCord had ripped his left shirt sleeve off and bandaged his wound.

Melba asked, "What's your poison, big man? It's on the house."

"Bourbon," Fargo answered.

McCord offered, "Now that I own this saloon, we were discussing the pros and cons about what to do with it. Fix it up, or burn it to the ground. What do you say, Fargo?"

They watched Fargo take a long pull from the bottle, then he said, "I think you ought to keep it. The flutist will—"

"Flutist?" McCord snorted. "What in hell is that?"

"A person who knows how to play a flute." He proceeded to describe a flute. He concluded by saying, "It's usually tootled by a woman."

"Why would I want a female flute player?" McCord wanted to know.

"To bring more peace and tranquillity to the neighborhood. A flutist plays soothing music." Fargo picked up his bottle and nodded for Melba to head for the back door.

She went to it eagerly.

When Melba opened the door, enough light spilled out for him to see wide planks, placed end to end, that formed a walkway leading to the door of a shack about ten paces distant, directly behind the saloon. She cautioned, "Don't slip and fall, big man. Don't want it getting hurt, do we?"

Now that she had alluded to it, he saw the gooey mud over which the planks stretched. She held his hand and led him safely to the shack.

He waited at the door while Melba lit a lamp. The small room had no windows. A bureau stood against a side wall, the bed against the other. The lamp was on the bureau.

Melba said, "It ain't much, but it is home. Come on in, big man."

Fargo had seen worse. At least she had a wooden floor. He stepped inside and tossed his hat in a corner. Melba stood beside the bureau and watched him remove the saddlebags from his shoulder and undo his gun belt and put both on the floor next to the bed and slip his

Colt under the pillow. He sat on the edge of the bed to pull off his shirt and boots.

"I'll help you get out of those Levi's," she suggested, coming across the room.

"And I'll help you with that dress," he mocked.

She was faster undoing buttons than he. Pulling open his fly, Melba reached in. Her sad eyes tried to smile as she whispered, "Nice. Oh, yes, my, oh, my, it is nice. And hot."

He worked the last button loose on the back of her dress. "Turn around, Melba." Reluctantly, she brought her hand out of his fly and turned. He rose and pulled the dress over her head and dropped it on his gun belt. She backed against his hardened member and wiggled her ass on it. He reached around the frail woman and teased her nipples.

Melba moaned, "That feels good. Makes me tingle all over, get good and hot. Sorry 'bout my boy's chest, but I don't want anything getting in my way."

He tweaked the nipples again, then pulled down his Levi's, bringing the underdrawers with them.

Melba turned and curled an arm around his strong neck, tilted her face up, and closed her eyes. Her breathing quickened when his hands went to her buttocks, grasped the slender cheeks, and raised her from the floor to kiss her.

As they kissed, her slim legs came up and locked around his waist. He put the head of his shaft between her hot, juicy lips, then backed her against the wall next to the door.

Her hot gasps filled his mouth as she murmured, "I have never . . . had it this way . . . before. Jesus, my head is already spinn . . ."

Fargo suddenly shoved and went deep.

Her eyes flew open. She broke the kiss and cried through clenched teeth, "Aaagh-aaagh! Damn, oh, damn."

He lifted her higher and sucked her big nipples and rolled each between his teeth.

Melba gulped and tightened her clamp around his waist. Pushing down, she captured his full length. Swaying on it, she moaned, "Jesus . . . oh, Jesus, that's so good. I have never had it so good before."

He met his thrusts by pulling down on her buttocks.

Each time he did Melba gasped loudly, "Oh . . . oh . . . oh, that's it . . . that's it. Go faster, big man . . . go faster."

Both were sweating profusely when he thrust deeply and held it there while throbbing out his flow. She lay her head on his shoulder and clutched his muscled back throughout his eruption. Only after he was spent did she loosen her leglock. Still entwined, Fargo carried Melba to the bed and gently lay her on it.

She sighed, "That was so good. I'll never forget you, big man. Or the unbelievable pleasure you gave me. I will—"

He put a finger to her lips to hush her. Lying next to her, he said, "Enough of that, now. It felt good to me, too. Snuggle up and go to sleep."

Turning on her side to face him, she lay her head on his powerful shoulder, sighed again, closed her eyes, and obeyed him.

Fargo drifted to sleep wondering if Ray and John Barrow were the pair in the hotel.

Smoke snapped his eyes open. He glanced at the lamp. The flame was low, but otherwise the lamp was normal, as it should be. He sniffed again to make sure he smelled smoke. He got out of bed and went to the door. Pushing it open, he saw dawn was breaking . . . and smoke billowing from the roof of the saloon and the glow of flames from across the street.

He shouted, "Wake up, Melba. We have to get out of here."

He was already pulling on his clothes when she roused and asked, "Why? Come back to bed."

"The town is on fire."

She bolted up. "The saloon?" she asked.

"Yes," he told her. "Get dressed and get out of here." He ran outside, slipped, and fell on the planks. Splashing facedown in the mud, he yelled, "Aw, shit."

"What did you say?" she hollered back.

He got up and ran around the saloon. The jail, feed

store, hotel, saloon—every structure except the general store and McCord's Trading Post—were on fire. The naked women were standing out in the street watching the hotel burn. Half-dressed men were running to their horses. McCord lay on his back in the street in front of the general store, a bottle gripped in one hand, the long handle of a blazing torch gripped in the other.

Running to him, Fargo glanced to the women and shouted, "Come with me. Take clothing from the general store." He pointed to the building.

He dropped to his knees beside McCord. Patting the mountain man's face, he asked, "Angus, can you hear me? It's Fargo, Angus." Even through the smell of smoke he could smell alcohol. McCord reeked from it.

McCord's eyes fluttered open. He blubbered, "Old buddy, old friend, I'm tired as hell. Resting. Been waiting for you. Was skinny Melba any good?"

"Angus, what in the blazes do you mean by torching the town?"

Angus brought the whiskey bottle to his mouth and drained the last few drops. Flinging the empty bottle away, he sat up and said, "I waited to burn down the general store."

Fargo knew the reason: Angus was waiting for the females to get clothing from it. But he didn't know McCord's reasoning for razing the whole town. "Why did you do this, Angus?"

McCord staggered to his feet. Looking at his handiwork, he slurred drunkenly, "Peace and tranquillity. By God, I was here first. I'm putting it back like it was. Peace and tranquillity." His head rolled sluggishly to face Fargo. Smiling, Angus said, "Magee and me got your pinto out back of the livery with horses for them females. Was Melba any good?"

"You already asked me that," Fargo answered. He realized what McCord was saying with reference to the six females; now that Vásquez and the others were dead, he wanted to level Beaver Pond to prevent another Castle from coming in and taking up where the last one left off. Pure and simple, the huge mountain man did not want to see any more naked young women taken captive.

He said, "You can put the torch to the general store after we come out."

Fargo walked into the store and found the women trying on dresses. Annie twirled to expand the hem on the bright-yellow dress she wore. "Looks good on me, huh, Mr. Fargo?" She smiled.

"Take it off," he said. "All of you take them off."

"Why?" Annie gasped.

"Because I'm taking all of you to Wagon Wheel Gap. It's a long trip. You will need Levi's and shirts. And find something—a bag, for instance—to hold foodstuffs while on the trail."

While they started looking at Levi's and shirts, he stepped to the sales counter and opened his saddlebags and started packing the big pockets with jerky, tins of beans, and other such items.

Draping the bulging saddlebags over one shoulder, he headed for the door, saying, "I'll see you ladies outside."

He found McCord turning over the five dead men with his foot.

"What are you doing, Angus?"

"Inspecting," he slurred.

"Inspecting for what?"

"Where I shot 'em. I was low on Joe the bartender. Never did like the sneaky bastard, anyhow. But I see I got the others where I aimed for."

"What are you going to do now that you have Beaver Pond all to yourself again?"

"Me and Magee talked about it. He's going into business with me. I asked him to. Magee and me, we get along. We figure on drifting on down to Acoma village and bringing back them twins. Blue Corn for me and Doe's Tail for him. I never did like scrawny women. The bone down there hurts like hell."

Fargo wanted to say Doe's Tail wasn't scrawny. Instead, he said, "Good choice, Angus. Just remember—don't bring back any peyote with you. Aftertaste, you know." He saw the Levi-clad women filing out of the store and said, "You can burn the store to the ground now. Are you going to make good the owner's losses?"

"Already have. Paid the Hacketts a thousand dollars.

Reba took it. She said they were ready to move the merchandise someplace else, anyhow."

Fargo was surprised to hear Angus had that much cash. He asked, "Er, though it's none of my business, I'm curious to know where you got the thousand. Want to tell me?"

"Sure. I don't mind telling you. I found it in Jack Castle's desk drawer in his office. One thousand, eight hundred, to be exact, not counting change. Then I looked in his wallet and pockets and found three hundred more. I'm flush, Fargo. Want some of it?"

"No, but I bet Melba could use part of it."

"Hell, I forgot all about her. Think what I got off Castle's body would be enough for Melba? She's skinny as hell, you know."

"She'd appreciate the three hundred."

McCord walked with him to the horses. They found Magee there watching his livery and blacksmith shop going up in flames. He had the stallion and six other horses saddled and ready for the trail. Angus staggered up to him, draped the wounded arm over his shoulder, and said, "Come on, partner, all that's left is the general store. After it goes, you and me can start listening to peace and tranquillity again."

As they walked to burn the store, Fargo saw Melba meet them. McCord fumbled in his pocket and brought out the money and handed it to her. She kissed both him and Magee several times, then headed for Fargo, who was already in his saddle. Fargo saw McCord and Magee dragging the backs of their hands across their mouths and cheeks where she'd kissed them.

Coming to Fargo, Melba said, "Angus just gave me three hundred dollars . . . for doing nothing! Said I was too bony to screw."

"Well, you're not. If you're coming with us, you'll have to ride bareback. Try the gray over there. She's the only one with reins."

One of the women pitched a spare pair of Levi's and a shirt to Melba and said, "He made us get out of the dresses."

Melba wasn't bashful. She stripped in sight of God and

everybody and got into the new clothes, which were too big for her. Grinning at Fargo, she suggested, "Airy as all get out, but they'll do."

He watched her mount up, then he led the way north, out of burning Beaver Pond, away from the massacre site.

At sunset, he halted them by a creek and made camp. While the women built a fire, he went downstream to hunt for fresh meat. Five doe followed by an eight-point buck came to the stream to drink. The deer were in clear view of his position on an upper limb of a whispering pine. He put the butt of the Sharps to his shoulder and his sights on the buck's heart and started applying pressure on the trigger. The rifle fired, the buck dropped, the doe fled.

Fargo returned to camp with the buck across his broad shoulders. Lowering it to the ground, he asked if anyone knew how to dress deer. Helga said she knew and would show the others how. Fargo went to his saddlebags and got the deer knife he'd fetched at the general store. He handed it to her, then sat to watch her work.

Annie stood with her back against a huge fir to watch. She removed her hat and shook her head so her long blond hair would flow down her back.

In that instant a rifle shot ripped the night.

6

A plume of dirt hopped up between Annie's feet.

Fargo was already diving toward her. He tackled her at the waist. His momentum knocked her away from the massive fir.

A second slug chewed into the tree trunk where Annie's heart had been a split second ago.

Screaming, the women scattered and ran into the veiling darkness. They plunged into dense undergrowth, out of the firelight.

Annie pummeled him, screaming hysterically, "Take your filthy hands off me. Help! Help! Somebody pull him off me."

Reluctantly, Fargo slapped her face and growled, "Shut up, Annie."

Holding her breath, she felt her cheek. He watched her panic-stricken expression suddenly change to unmitigated fear.

Gripping her wrists, he rolled to one side, nodded to the raw-white spot left by the missing bark on the trunk, and said, "That greasy spot was meant for your heart, young lady." He told her to stay down, that he was going after the assailant.

Fargo drew his Colt. He moved swiftly among the trees to the creek, waded it, and crouched under a willow to look for the rifleman. Painted dull yellow-orange by the flames of the fire, he saw the vague shape of an outcrop high on the slope directly across from the fire. He approached cautiously, silently, and got into position above the outcrop. He saw no rifleman, but he did hear two horses pounding down the far side of the slope. He holstered the Colt and went down to the outcrop.

Feeling around in soil where he reckoned the rifleman had been, he found two shell casings. Standing, he shouted, "All right, ladies, you can come out now. They're gone." And he muttered to himself, "For the time being."

Coming down the slope, he saw the females weren't all that sure the rifleman, or riflemen, had left. They moved cautiously out of the darkness into the firelight, their eyes widened from fear. Annie Hogg wasn't among them.

Fargo went to the undergrowth to get her. She had worked her way deep into it. Annie's body lay in the fetal position. When he touched her, she screamed, "No. Please don't kill me. Please don't."

"It's me, Fargo," he told her.

Gasping, she clutched him and sobbed, "I'm so afraid, so scared."

He cradled her in his arms and carried her next to the fire, lowered her to sit on the ground. Then he explained, "We have to leave this place. Douse the light, forget the buck. It's Annie Hogg they are after. This makes three times they've tried to take her life. First, Vásquez, then the two men at the hotel, and now those same two dry-gulchers."

"Who are they?" Ruth Adcock asked. "Why do they want to kill Annie?"

"I don't know who or why," Fargo answered, "although I have my suspicions in regard to whom." He glanced at Annie and added, "She doesn't know why, and I'm still trying to figure it out."

Fargo knew by the way they stared at Annie Hogg that they viewed her as a dangerous liability to be around.

Helga Emerson confirmed his belief when she finally said, "No offense, Annie, but we'd appreciate it if you would sleep apart from us and ride last in line. We have ourselves to look out for."

Melba dropped to her knees and hugged Annie. Melba chastened the other women angrily, "I can't believe what I just heard. Of all the things to say! Why, you're a bunch of no-good bitches." She kissed Annie's cheek and said, "Well, honey, I'll sleep next to you . . . with you, in fact. And we'll ride right beside each other."

Fargo said, "Douse the fire, then mount up." He

stepped to his stallion and snugged the saddle's cinch strap. As he did, he told them, "Annie rides next to me. She can bed down anywhere she pleases. That's the way it's going to be." He got into the saddle.

The fire was put out. Nothing more was said. He nudged the pinto to walk. They followed single-file—all, that is, except Melba and Annie, who rode side by side at the rear of the column.

After riding about ten miles Fargo halted the procession among aspens on a slope. Dismounting, he said, "We sleep here. No fire, though. Annie, spread your bedroll next to mine."

"No," she snapped in a testy tone. "I've had enough of you men pawing me. I'll sleep near Melba."

And that confirmed what Fargo had suspected: Vásquez and his men had taken all the women forcibly after the massacre. She had been hurt and no longer trusted any man. Annie Hogg, like all the others, he told himself, would have to be handled gently. He said, "Suit yourself." He untied his bedroll, took it to the tree line downhill, and spread it between two aspens. As always, he stripped naked before lying down to sleep. He drifted into sleep looking up at constellations long familiar to him.

Annie's piercing scream jarred his eyes open. His hand flew to the Colt as he bolted to his feet . . . and ran into a sapling. All of the women were screaming as he shook his head to clear it of stars. Charging up the slope, he yelled, "I'm coming, I'm coming."

He got to them about the same time his night vision returned. Some were running helter-skelter, buck-naked. Others were climbing trees. Annie just sat and led the screaming. Five black bear cubs were the cause of the pandemonium. Three were chasing after those on foot, two were following women up the trunks.

Fargo uncocked his Colt and picked up a branch. He started switching the bears' rumps, those climbing the trees first. After briefly taking the blistering swats, the two bears dropped to the ground and fled, yelping. "Come to my voice, girls," he yelled over the screams.

Henrietta jumped on his back and locked her legs

around him. Fargo blistered a bear's behind when it raced by. He caught Martha by her arm and swung her high into the air, swatting the bear that was chasing her at the same time. Both bears ran away yelping.

The fifth bear had Helga cornered behind a big aspen. Fargo crept up behind the cub and grabbed its rump fur and roared like a lion. The playful bear jumped a foot off the ground and came down running, stumbling, yelping into the night.

Annie was still screaming hysterically. Fargo broke his gentle-handling vow, went to her, and slapped her. She stopped screaming instantly. He told them, "Go back to bed," and felt a hand grasp his member.

Melba whispered, "You want me in your bedroll, big man?"

"Not tonight," he answered, willing his manhood not to rise. He peeled her hand off it and walked down the slope.

Reclining, he noticed the Big Dipper was in the four-o'clock position. He went back to sleep wondering what would happen next.

Annie gasping, "Snake," awakened him an hour later.

He pulled on his underdrawers this time before going to see about her problem. "Where is the snake?" he asked.

"It's, it's in my bed, my bedroll," she whispered.

"How big?" he asked.

"Real big," she answered.

By this time, everybody was awake and around the bedroll, but at a safe distance, ready to spring back.

He asked, "Where is it?"

"All over me. I think its head or tail is, is, between . . . Oh, God, between my breasts."

He felt her forehead and brought back a sweaty palm. "Listen carefully," he began. "I'm going to reach in and yank it out."

"No," she hissed, then whispered, "It might bite me."

"Snakes coil before they strike. Is it coiled?"

"Yes . . . No. I don't know," she gasped.

"Well, do you feel it on your, er, crotch?"

"No. It's on my left thigh."

Fargo eased his right hand inside the bedroll and walked his fingers over her breastbone. She was nude, all right. "Don't move a muscle," he cautioned, "when I touch your breast. Above all, do not scream. Do you hear me, Annie? I said, do not scream."

She nodded slightly and gulped.

He slid his palm over her right nipple.

She screamed and shot out of the bedroll, leaving him holding the snake's tail. It instantly coiled around his forearm. He pulled his arm out slowly and saw it was a friendly king snake.

The women fell back, gasping.

Fargo walked a short distance and held his arm to the ground. The king snake released its grip on his forearm and slipped away. He went back and told them, "Okay, girls, it's time for us to be on our way."

"I couldn't go back to sleep if my life depended on it," Melba admitted.

"Me neither," Inez and Eva echoed.

"What kind of a snake was it?" Annie asked.

"A big rattler," Fargo lied. "You're lucky to be alive."

Annie Hogg fainted.

He left Melba to revive her and went to his bedding, rolled it up, and sat on it to pull on the rest of his clothes. Pausing, he looked skyward thoughtfully, then asked, "Why me, oh, Lord? Why me?"

At sunup he halted the weary procession on open ground in a wide valley. Most of their chins rested on their collarbones.

"Get off those horses. Make a small fire. This snake-handler needs coffee." When they remained in their saddles and just stared at him, he shouted forcibly, "Now!"

They were quick to obey.

Fargo sat on a large, smooth boulder nearby. Now and then he glanced at the coffeepot, but mostly he looked at the valley floor. The aroma of brewing coffee mingled with scents of lupine, snowy green gentian, and pink plumes. A path of brilliant fireweed painted the floor on his right. Indian paintbrushes grew here in profusion, bees already at work among them. Tall sunflowers were awakening, turning their orange-and-yellow-and-brown faces to the sun, which peeked over the snow-capped Montezuma's Peak on his left.

He was immersed in the carpet of wildflowers and his thoughts drifted to Angus McCord burning Beaver Pond. He mused inwardly, Angus knew what he was doing: he was fighting back the encroachment of civilization, the expanding western frontier.

And those thoughts gave way to the immediate problem. His hand dropped into the right Levi's pocket and slowly withdrew the pouch of nuggets given to him by Roscoe Hogg. He dumped the nuggets in his palm. Fingering them absentmindedly, he wondered where the old man got the nuggets, and when. He wished that Hogg hadn't died before he got the chance to ask.

One thing was clear, though: Roscoe and his brother were en route to Wagon Wheel Gap. Annie had said they were to meet her cousin, Tessa, who was arriving by stagecoach. He would ask Annie whether Wagon Wheel Gap was where the Hoggs planned on settling, or if they meant to move on to another place.

Focusing on the nuggets, he wondered if they had anything to do with the attempts on Annie Hogg's life.

Melba, clearing her throat, broke into his thoughts. "Coffee's made, big man."

Nodding, he returned the nuggets to the pouch and stuck it in his pocket. He slid off the boulder and walked with the saloon girl to the fire.

Helga handed him a tin cup of the steaming brew and asked, "How much farther do we have to go, Mr. Fargo?" She watched him blow softly on his coffee to cool it a tad.

Finally, he answered, "At this slow pace, I'd say mid-afternoon tomorrow. Providing there are no more interruptions by big, mean bears or . . ." He hesitated briefly, glanced over the rim of his cup at Annie, then finished, "Big snakes."

Annie glowered at him, then turned her back to him.

He drank two cups of coffee. Cleaning out grounds with a finger, he stood and said, "Mount up, ladies."

They rode through the serene valley of wildflowers to

a tight gap in a rocky cliff. "Careful, ladies," he cautioned. "Don't scrape your—"

"Ow," Melba suddenly hollered. "Damn!"

He glanced over his shoulder and saw her rubbing her left knee. The Ovaro twisted through the shadowy zigzag split in the rocks and broke out into sunlight. A narrow, rocky canyon where nothing green grew lay before them.

Rounding a sharp bend, Fargo saw a king snake easing over rocks. On top of one basked an unsuspecting rattlesnake. He reined to a halt and motioned the women forward.

Melba asked quietly, "What is it?" Glancing around, she added with a trace of concern, "You see them waiting for a shot at Annie?"

He pointed to the snakes camouflaged in the rocks. "Watch what happens."

As he spoke, the king lunged for the coiled rattler, whose rattles instantly started buzzing. The yard-long rattler struck, sinking its venomous fangs into the king's body. When the rattler recoiled to strike again, the king was swifter. The poisonous snake's head was suddenly gripped by the king's mouth. The rattler thrashed trying to get free. The king kept its grip on the head and coiled around the rattler's body and began constricting, squeezing it to death. The two snakes became entwined and fell to lower rocks. Slowly, the rattler's body lost all life and became limp. Still gripping its head, the king snake uncoiled from around the dead rattler. It pulled the rattler straight, to its full length, then stretched its own four-foot body straight out. The king unhinged its jaws and slowly started to devour its meal.

Fargo said, "It's a king snake."

Melba muttered, "Will it die, too?"

"No," he answered. "The king is the only snake immune to venom. That's why it is called the king snake. It will take a little time, but the king will swallow the rattler whole, then go to a shady spot to digest its meal, scales, bones, rattles, and all." He looked at Annie and commented, "That was a king inside your bedroll. You had no way of knowing—neither did I—but it wouldn't have bitten you. Kings are one of the friendliest snakes around."

"Well, it was very friendly with me," they heard Annie mumble. "So were you, Mr. Fargo."

"Uh, huh," he muttered. In a stronger voice, he asked them, "Ladies, what have you just learned?"

"That snakes eat snakes?" Henrietta asked.

Nodding, Fargo explained, "You have learned that the deadliest of snakes, like deadly men, can be killed quick as a wink when you aren't afraid and remain calm, keeping your eye on the target. In this instance, the deadly rattler's head. In regard to deadly men, you keep your eyes fixed on theirs. Come along, ladies. School's out."

They picked their way through the rocky terrain and left the canyon to find a mountain forest of blue spruce at the far end. At midday, Fargo found a shallow, gurgling stream fed by a series of waterfalls. He dismounted, stretched, and said, "We'll stop here to eat. No fire, though."

Melba looked at the waterfall. Smiling, she announced, "I don't know about you other women, but I'm taking a bath."

They watched her start shucking clothes as she walked to the waterfalls. By the time Melba got to the water she was nude. The women cast furtive glances at Fargo that implied they wanted to bathe also, but not in his presence.

Through an easy grin, he told them, "Hell, ladies, you haven't got anything I haven't seen before. But if it will make you more comfortable, I'll go downstream and sit on a rock."

He started to walk away. Helga stopped him in midstride when she said, "Mr. Fargo, you don't have to do that. You've seen our nakedness before, hasn't he, ladies?"

"But you haven't seen mine," he reminded. "Thanks, anyhow, but I want to take a dip, too. I think it best for me to go downstream."

Downstream he found a pool, out of sight to the females, but not out of hearing. Pulling off his clothes, he listened to the squeals and giggles as they frolicked in the ice-cold water. Holding his breath, he plunged into the pool. He swam underwater, going back and forth across the pool several times before he surfaced at the far bank. Sensing somebody or something was watching him, he began scanning among the trees. He saw nobody. He turned around to check on the other side.

Annie sat with her knees drawn to her chest and arms wrapped around her shins. She was fully clothed, staring at him, as though about to make a profound statement. He waited.

Finally, she said, "Mr. Fargo, I detest you."

When he laughed and started to speak, she hurried to continue. "Please, don't speak until I'm finished. Your callousness and your overall attitude, your high-handed ways, are what is repugnant to me."

She hadn't learned anything from the snakes, he thought, but said instead, "Do go on."

"At the same time I must suffer you a while longer, which is to say I am at your mercy. I need you, Mr. Fargo."

"Need?" he interjected.

"Oh, no. Don't get it in your head that I lust for your body."

He didn't think she implied that. But she did. She was the one who broached the subject of lust. It was on her mind, whether or not she was conscious of the fact. He waited.

She continued, "I don't need you in that way. I don't need any man. I find myself in need of your knowledge of this particular part of the country. Accordingly, I'm prepared to make a bargain with you, pending my cousin agrees, of course."

"Bargain? What bargain?"

She stood and started pacing. "First, it is necessary for you to know some of the background information, why I am here to meet Tessa.

"My father and Uncle Charlie returned home—Lynchburg, Virginia—after prospecting for gold here in Colorado."

"And they found some," Fargo broke in.

"Yes. They were jubilant. Anyhow, that was last October, when they returned home. They said the only reason they left when they did was because of lack of supplies to sustain them during the long winter. They had just discovered the gold when, as they put it, 'The first snow flew and forced us to leave.' "

"Smart move. Go on."

"They brought back four bags of nuggets. Uncle Charlie had two and my father two. My father gave you one of them. Uncle Charlie owed money to Mrs. Abigail Fincher's Finishing School for Young Ladies in Boston, which Tessa was attending. So he reduced his nuggets to cash. My father did the same with one of his bags."

"Your mothers had to be pleased with this newfound wealth," Fargo remarked.

"They're both deceased, Mr. Fargo. I lived with my Aunt Phyllis on my mother's side of the family, and worked in Mr. Harper's factory as a weaver. Papa got me out of there and told me I would never have to work again."

Fargo leapfrogged over her background information, saying, "So, you returned to Colorado with your father and uncle. Your cousin would come later."

"That's correct. After she completed her schooling."

"Where is the gold located?"

"I don't rightly know. That's where you come in. All I know is they had a mine. They named it Rainbow's End, meaning where they found a pot of gold."

"Too bad they didn't have enough time to work it dry."

"That's precisely what Papa said."

"You said you didn't rightly know the location of the mine. That implies you have a rough idea where it is. Enlighten me."

She stopped pacing and faced him. "And that information, Mr. Fargo, will have to wait until after Tessa and I talk."

"You don't trust me?"

"Exactly."

He grinned and reminded her, "You also admitted you were at my mercy. Young lady, you're mistaken. You are free to leave me anytime you wish. In the meantime, I promised your father I would look after you, meaning I would get you to your destination. I keep my promises. I have no interest in gold. I enjoy my freedom to roam where I please. Gold would prevent that. So, suit yourself about not telling me what might happen, where we might go after you chat with your cousin. Now, I don't hear the others squealing, which means they have left the water. I'm about to do likewise, so if you don't want to see me naked, you had better get out of sight."

Annie Hogg spun immediately and strode out of view.

He lay on the bank in the sunlight to dry off while assessing what she had revealed. One thing was damn clear, he concluded: a person unknown had learned of the mine. And the only person other than the six females to survive the massacre was the one who met Silas and the others on the knoll. Did Roscoe and/or Charlie take the person into their confidence? Or did Annie Hogg? he mused. A lover perhaps? Either way the person was out to kill, to silence her forever. The person had to be a man, he reasoned. Or did he? he quickly asked himself. A woman could have just as easily hired those dry-gulchers to kill her, he decided. But what woman? The only woman he'd seen when he had arrived in Beaver Pond was Melba. Hmmmmm . . .

He considered the four women, not the girls, he and McCord had found in Diablo Canyon. Could one have been taking the old man or his brother into the bushes at night? It happened more often than anyone might imagine, even Annie. Did one of the brothers tell the mine's location to the woman? As luck would have it, the Apaches attacked and massacred the source of her information. As bad luck would have it, the Apaches captured her . . . and Annie Hogg, the only other person left who knew anything about the mine.

Fargo could imagine the woman biding her time, waiting to get Annie alone and murder her. The females of the species are far more treacherous and deadly than the male, he reminded himself. Then McCord and I showed up and destroyed her plan. We took her to Beaver Pond, where I was with her all the time except . . . except . . .

He thought back and considered the time. Sure, he concluded, she had the time. After installing them in the hotel, I went to the saloon. The two drifters, Ray and Frank Barrow, ducked out during the card game. McCord and the others took Jack Castle to the hanging tree. I went with them. Then Ott and the other three made their appearance. After the gunfight, I heard the women screaming and ran to the hotel. That gave her the time to get with the pair who tried to kill Annie. Fargo decided the pair was none other than the Barrow brothers.

But something wasn't squaring in his mind. None of the women knew the Barrow brothers. Moreover, none of them had the means to hire killers. And that brought Fargo back to the unknown survivor. He didn't know the survivor's gender—not that it mattered. He concluded the person had got with Roscoe or Charlie back in Lynchburg. Without Annie's knowing it, a deal had been struck, and that person learned the mine's location. He or she had hired the gunmen, probably the Barrows, although Fargo wasn't all that positive. After all, he hadn't seen the dry-gulchers' faces, so doubt existed.

One thing was damn sure: if he had figured correctly, then Tessa shared her cousin's danger. He quit thinking about it, got up, dressed, and went back to the others. He found them dressed and in their saddles. Good, he thought, and got into his.

7

After breakfast the next morning Fargo suggested Annie and he take a short stroll, he had something to say to her in private. Walking under a canopy of whispering pine needles, he questioned her about the possibility of her father or uncle getting with somebody back in Lynchburg and making an arrangement without her or Tessa's knowledge.

She shook her head, said, "No," and explained that none of the people on the wagon train was from Lynchburg, or from anywhere near the city. She went on to tell where each was from, concluding with "The first time Papa and I and Uncle Charlie met any of them was on the east bank of the Mississippi. They were all good, decent people wanting so very much to make a new life for themselves. You're wrong, Mr. Fargo, thinking the other person who survived wants to kill me and my cousin. That's simply out of the realm of reasoning."

"Then, how do you explain it?"

"What?"

"The attempts on your life."

She stopped walking. "I don't know. Maybe they hate my looks."

"I think not. Whoever they are, they know about Rainbow's End."

He decided they were getting nowhere by discussing it. The answer, if there was to be one, would have to wait until after her cousin's arrival. They walked back and broke camp.

That afternoon they rode into Wagon Wheel Gap. The town was built in a wide bend in the otherwise narrow valley rimmed by beautiful mountains. The valley meandered, following the flow of a branch of the Rio Grande. Fargo saw the Gap had grown in size and population since he had seen it two years ago. He attributed the growth to increasing worry about civil war between the north and south. Folks from both sides of the Mason-Dixon line were pulling up stakes and moving west to escape both the known and the unknown. The pity of it was, he thought, where decent, God-fearing people went, the rotten element was sure to follow.

Passing the livery, he saw that old man Jonas Record, the owner, had built a new and expanded corral. Wedged between a new bank and a land office, both of which Fargo hadn't seen before, stood Miss Candy's Saloon. He noticed Candace Beaulieu had given the saloon a fresh coat of gleaming white paint. Two saloon girls waved to him from the balcony. He tipped his hat to them.

The Gap fairly bristled with commerce. A glass-windowed delivery wagon was just leaving from out in front of the general store. As it left, a surrey parked. Two Bucks County hay wagons and a Studebaker farm wagon stood waiting at the feed store. Two other surreys were parked in front of the little bank. Fargo counted six Conestogas parked in a sea of alpine forget-me-nots across the river. He watched an Owensboro mountain rig with oversized brakes drawn by six mules coming toward him. Citizens were walking on the porches in front of shops or crossing the street.

He led the women straight to the two-story hotel and told them to dismount, that this was the end of the line. Annie and Melba hitched their horses next to his stallion.

Draping his saddlebags over his left shoulder, Fargo took Annie by the arm to help her up the front steps.

She jerked away, slipped, and fell.

In that instant a shot was fired.

The slug thudded into a board on the top step.

The women screamed and ran inside the hotel.

Fargo had his Colt drawn and cocked in a flash. He backed into Annie to protect her, to shield her with his body if necessary, and quick-scanned the far side of the street to hopefully spot a smoking gun. He saw none.

Pedestrians cleared the street. Some simply ducked into shops, others got behind something solid.

Fargo said, "Annie, run into the Summerhill Café. It's on your left. Next to the hotel. Go!"

When she ran, five evenly spaced bullets stitched the front of the hotel. Fargo saw the muzzle flashes winkle from the slightly opened door to Buster Hix's Barber Shop. He swung the Colt and squeezed the trigger three times. The glass in the door shattered. Before the first shard hit the porch, Fargo was running toward the door. Blasting inside the barber shop, he glimpsed Buster's body on the floor behind the barber's chair, a razor in his hand.

Buster groaned, "Out back."

Three strides put Fargo at the back door. Standing at the wall next to it, he kicked it open.

Two bullets instantly shattered the shop's front windowpane.

Fargo crouched and reloaded, then twisted into the doorway and fired an intimidating round.

Ray and John Barrow peered over the rims of their round wooden bathtubs. Ray said, "He went over the fence."

Three tall modesty fences enclosed the bath area. "Which one?" Fargo asked, scanning all three.

"The back," Frank answered.

Fargo pressed over it. Outbuildings, outhouses, and sheds mostly stood behind shops. He scanned them for any sign of movement as he sprinted to the end of the fence. Peering down the scant space separating the barber shop and bank, he saw nobody. He ran to the saloon next to the bank. The back door was ajar.

He yanked it wide open, his Colt up and ready to fire. Heavy shadows greeted him in the short hallway. The door to Miss Candy's office was closed. So was the door to her apartment across the hall. But the door leading into the saloon was parted by an inch. He stepped to it. Easing the door open by a head's width, he looked inside the saloon. Everybody except Herbert Wilson, the bartender, stood looking out front windows. He holstered the Colt and stepped into the saloon.

Herbie glanced at him. "What's all the ruckus about, Fargo?" he asked nonchalantly.

Fargo knew Herbie was accustomed to gunplay. After ten years of bartending, Wilson was no longer alarmed by shoot-outs—he saw at least three a week, either in saloons or in the street in front of them. Herbert Wilson was a year older than Fargo. The stocky man stood five-eight, had clear, piercing dark eyes and hair that matched. The corners of Herbie's lips were upturned in a perpetual hint of a grin. It was deceptive, as many rowdy customers had learned. Wilson was tougher, much tougher than the perpetual grin presented. He would vault over the bar and take on any man, slugging away with his hamlike fists. Herbie had the knuckle scars to prove it.

Fargo asked, "Anybody come through this door in the last few minutes?"

"Not that I saw," Herbie replied. He finished drying the shot glass he held and brought from under the bar a fresh bottle of bourbon.

As he poured from it into a glass, Fargo stepped to the bar.

"Noticed you ride in and hitch in front of the hotel," Herbie began. "What's with all the women you brought to town?"

First Fargo drank from the glass. Licking his lips, he answered, "Survivors from a massacre near Beaver Pond. Gotta go, Herbie." He put a two-bit piece on the bar.

Wilson shoved it back, saying, "The first one is on the house."

Fargo nodded. Herbie watched him walk outside and amble to the café.

Dorothy and Pete Henderson were behind the long counter. Their daughter, LaDonna, was in the kitchen. She leaned into the doorway behind the counter and smiled at Fargo. Annie sat on a stool at the end of the counter. She glanced over her shoulder at him.

Pete asked, "Did you catch him? The young lady told us what happened."

Dorothy poured Fargo a cup of steaming coffee.

"No, he got away." He sat beside Annie. Looking at her, he said, "You all right? Nerves calmed down?"

"I'm fine."

Sipping from the cup, he muttered, "You're lucky he's a lousy shot. If the bastard wasn't so focused on killing you, he would have waited around to shoot me out of the way. Clumsy of him." He looked at Dorothy and asked, "Is it all right with you if Annie stays in the kitchen with LaDonna while I see to the women in the hotel?"

"Sure," Pete answered. "No bother at all. LaDonna would appreciate her company."

"I don't have any say-so?" Annie snapped.

"No," Fargo growled. "Now get up and go in the kitchen." He watched her swell up and glower at him. But she did like he said.

Fargo shot a wink Dorothy's way. He put a dime on the counter and left.

Entering the hotel, he saw the females sitting in chairs. Nodding to them, he stepped to the registration counter behind which stood a haggard-faced older man who said, "I don't cotton to troublemakers, mister." He glanced to the women and added, "Especially, improper women and ragamuffin kids."

Fargo ignored the man's remark. "Need two rooms for the *ladies* and *children*."

"The hotel is full," the man persisted.

Fargo glanced to the room keys hanging on a rack and saw several doubles, which suggested vacancies. Noting two double-key room numbers, he said evenly, "We'll take numbers six and eight. Make it snappy. I'm in a hurry."

"Sir, I just informed you there are no vacancies. Are you deaf?"

Fargo went behind the counter. Shoving the startled man out of his way, he removed the keys to six and eight from their pegs. Motioning the women to follow him, he said, "Wait here, Melba. I'll get to you later."

He installed Henrietta, Helga, and Inez in room six. Martha and the other two women in eight. Handing each twenty dollars, he said, "This is for decent clothes. I'll pay for a two-week stay in the hotel and arrange for you to eat at the Summerhill Café till you get settled in. Look after Martha. I will check on you before I leave town. It's been a pleasure, ladies." Touching the brim of his hat, he bid them good day.

In the lobby, he slapped twenty dollars on the registration counter, told the trembling clerk he was prepaying for the rooms, then led Melba outside and went to the café.

He gave Dorothy forty dollars and told her that was for meals for the six females, then he called Annie out of the kitchen and led her and Melba to Miss Candy's Saloon.

Annie balked at the double doors. "Mr. Fargo, I'm not setting foot in this place. No proper lady would."

He shoved her inside and said, "After all you have been through, I promise this place will be a paradise on earth."

Men lined the bar. More sat around the ten tables, drinking and playing cards. Miss Candy's three shapely saloon girls—Roxanne, Fifi, and Wanda—were busy serving drinks to the card players. Henry "the Eighth" Morgan, Miss Candy's black piano player, sat at the ivories, banging out a lively tune. All cut their eyes to the new arrivals standing just inside the swinging doors of the haze-blue, smoke-filled room. Fargo stepped to the bar and asked Wilson where to find Miss Candy.

"She's in her apartment," Wilson told him. "Go on back and surprise her. I know she will be pleased to see you again."

Fargo nodded for the two women to follow him. Melba was in her element, Fargo saw. The skinny brunette was beaming and resisting the urge to fondle the men's crotches. He noticed her fingers literally begged to touch. On the other hand, Annie walked stiffly, her hazel eyes focused on the floor.

He led them to Miss Candy's door and rapped on it three times, paused, and rapped a fourth time. The door opened.

Candace Beaulieu smiled hugely as she embraced him tightly to her. She whispered, "Lover man, I thought you would never get back." The petite, full-figured woman raised on tiptoe and kissed him openmouthed, hungrily, as though a long, miserable drought was finally over, as though it might suddenly come back. She came by it naturally—a gift from her mother, Stella—as she did her profession.

Before Candace was born, Stella Beaulieu's constant preaching sin and salvation chased her unborn baby's father out of Atlanta. Stella discovered she couldn't live with or without the rugged man. After Candace was born, Stella followed him to New Jersey. Bradford Charmaine refused to let Stella live with him or use his name. He failed to contribute to their support and denied paternity. However, he did allow Stella to take a room next door to his. That arrangement let him escape her Bible-thumping ways, as well as the disorder accompanying all children, and at the same time give him instant access to Stella's wild, fiery lovemaking.

Baby Candace grew up being somewhat cared for by the owner of the house, Mrs. O'Mally, and her young daughter, Erin, who was three years older than Candace. Candace's mother worked as a seamstress in a sail loft on the waterfront nearby, within walking distance.

When Candace was fourteen—and already blossoming out—Erin began spending more and more time at the Schooner, a waterfront whorehouse catering to sailors and longshoremen. Erin introduced her young, platinum blonde—the hair was a natural color—friend to sex. The madame wouldn't allow Candace to work. But where there was a will, there was a way, and Erin and Candace's wills were strong and eager. Candace found the way to climb the outside wall and get in through Erin's second-story window.

It lasted two years before Madame Irene Fogerty found out and ran the two off. Candace wasn't paying the angry madame her cut; Candace and Erin divided Candace's earnings, which were considerable. At Candace's suggestion they moved west, to St. Louis, and became saloon girls. The pair were exceedingly popular, with Candace being the favorite, due to her diminutive size, curly hair, baby face, and big breasts.

Five years later two major things happened in Candace's life: Erin got married and left her for good; and an old man, who adored being between Candy's legs, died and left her five thousand dollars.

Candy promptly built the first Miss Candy's Saloon, which she operated successfully for five years. At age twenty-six Candy moved farther west, to Denver, where she bought another saloon and named it the same as the first. Miss Candy and her exciting bosom and fast-moving crotch were the talk of Denver.

Four years of living fast had exhausted Miss Candy. She sold her saloon, saying she was ready to settle down. She moved farther west, to Wagon Wheel Gap. The retirement lasted six months before the tuggings in her groin simply became overpowering and she established her third Miss Candy's Saloon.

She met Skye Fargo a year later, and instantly fell in love with him. The big, soft-spoken man was her first and only love. Now she had him back in her arms, kissing him.

Annie cleared her throat.

Frowning, Miss Candy pulled back to look around Fargo's broad chest and saw the two women. Then she cut questioning ice-blue eyes up to his lake-blues.

He grinned and allayed her fears. "No, I'm not married to either. I need your help, Candy. There's been a problem at the Pond."

"Oh? Angus McCord? Is he with you?" She glanced behind Fargo.

He chuckled. "No. The last time I saw him, he was blind-drunk. Angus and Magee were burning the place to the ground. I want to talk to you about these two females." He turned to face them and suggested, "Ladies, if you will wait in the hall?" He closed the door.

Crossing to a wing-back chair, he sat. Candace did too, in his lap. Curling an arm around his neck she fingered his black hair and asked, "Well? Are you going to tell me?"

"The tall skinny one—"

Her pulling a lock of his hair cut him off as she said, "No, Fargo, I meant were you going to say you love me. I've waited so long, lover."

She was making him uncomfortable. In fact, arousing

him. He willed his stiffened member to soften and answered her question by saying, "First, we talk business."

"And after?" she whispered.

"Afterward, I'll get two bottles of bourbon from Herbie and cuddle with you."

"It's a deal," she said, and got out of his lap to light up a ready-roll. Standing at the bureau, she asked, "Well, I'm waiting."

"As I was about to say, the skinny one is Melba. I got her out of the saloon in the nick of time before McCord torched it."

"Jack Castle's place?" she inquired. "That card-cheating bastard deserved it."

"Yes, well, McCord ended up killing Jack. Melba needs a job. Will you . . ."

"Give her one?" Candace finished his question. "Honey, you're asking a lot, a whole lot from me. Why, the woman is skinny as a rail, bones poking out all over her body, knobby-kneed, not to mention the flattest chest I've ever laid eyes on. Really, Fargo."

"I know, I know," he began. "Look at it this way: Melba would be perfect for your chicken-eating Methodist clientele."

"Chicken-eating Methodists?" Candace shot him a frown.

"The closer the bone, the sweeter the meat?" he explained.

He watched her shoulders sag as she sighed, "I'll give her a try. The shapely blonde?"

"She's straight—arrow-straight," Fargo added, "but used."

"By you?"

"No." He proceeded to tell Candace about the circumstances under which he became involved with Annie Hogg, then said, "She needs a safe place to stay. Somebody's out to kill the young lady. I can't keep my eye on her all the time."

"Uh, huh, I bet you would. Okay, I have three spare bedrooms upstairs. Skinny Melba gets one, little Annie can stay in one of the other two. Will that solve your immediate—*our* immediate problem?"

He went to Candace and hugged her. He started to say, "That will be perfect," but she stopped him with a wet, passionate kiss.

Breaking the kiss, he peeled her arms from around him and muttered, "Business first."

Smoothing her red dress, Miss Candy stepped to the door and yanked it open. She was all business when she said, "Melba, I'm giving you work. I'm also changing your name, to, to . . . Erin, God forbid. Chicken-eating Methodists?"

Melba, now Erin, grunted, "Huh?"

Miss Candy sighed heavily and said, "That's what he claims." Turning to Annie, she said, "Honey, you can stay in an upstairs room, too."

"Honey? Honey?" Annie blurted. "Don't you dare compare me with, with—"

"Saloon girls?" Miss Candy helped. "Call us what we are, young lady. We're pure whores. Sluts for rent by the minute, hour, or all night. Don't worry, you will not have to spread your legs and receive the thrill of clasping them around a man's waist, a man like Fargo."

Fargo stepped to the door and said, "Annie, it's just for as long until your cousin arrives. You'll be safe here. Nobody will bother you. I promise."

Annie's shoulders sagged in capitulation. She mumbled, "Mr. Fargo, I didn't think you know what you're doing, but I'll go along with you."

"Fine," Miss Candy replied. "Like he said, you will be safe here. Come along, ladies, and I'll show you to your rooms."

Fargo tagged along behind them. Going up the stairs, he noticed Erin kept glancing over her bony shoulders, eyeing the customers eagerly. Annie's rolling rump brought fascinated looks from the men as they mentally undressed her. "Miss Candy's bringing fresh meat to the table, boys," Fargo heard one of the men say.

"All you chicken-livered Methodists form a line," Fargo heard Miss Candy say, chuckling.

Candace moved Erin into the room first. Erin immediately went to the curtained window and looked out, saying joyously, "My very own window. Golly, gee, this is great."

"Well, darling, you can look out at it from the bed. Now, I don't want to see you downstairs until after I buy new dresses for you . . . and do something with that horrible-looking hair. Henry the Eighth will bring your meals. One of the girls will show you where you can have a bath."

They left Erin looking out the window and went to the room Candace had selected for Annie. A yellow canopied bed dominated the room. It had matching sheets, pillowcases, and bedcovers. Sheer white curtains hung over the window. Soft brown throw rugs lay beside the bed.

"Like it?" Miss Candy asked.

"It will do," Annie muttered.

Miss Candy answered with a laugh. Walking from the room, she said, "Don't kid me, Annie. It's the best goddamn room you have ever been in. I treat my girls to the finest."

"I'm not one of your girls," Annie barked.

"Have it your way," Miss Candy said, going through the doorway.

Fargo told Annie, "Lock the door. Don't let anybody in except Miss Candy or me. And stay away from the window."

"I know," she snapped. "I can look out it while flat on my back in the cute yellow bed."

Fargo made no reply. He walked out in the hall and shut the door. He waited until he heard her lock it, then went down to the saloon and asked Herbie for two bottles of bourbon.

Grinning, Herbie told him, "Miss Candy's already picked them up."

"Oh, has she, now?" Nodding, Fargo headed for her door and gave his personal knock on it.

"Come on in, lover man," he heard her say.

Opening the door, he saw Miss Candy stretched out on the bed, naked and waiting for him with open arms.

She watched him remove his gun belt and drop it in the wing-back chair. He pitched his Colt onto the bed. She knew to tuck it under a pillow. Watching him pull off his boots, she purred, "God, but I love watching you undress. You realize, don't you, lover, that you have a beautiful body? Well, you do. All of your hard muscles—I do mean hard—excite me. Take your time undressing. I've waited so long to feel your body pressing against mine that I can wait a minute or two longer."

Loosening his belt, he remembered Marie Mercier's silver compact. She watched him come and stand beside the bed. He grinned smugly.

Candace said, "Well, don't just stand there with your hand in your pocket. Are you wanting me to undo the buttons on your fly?" Her right hand reached for the buttons.

Fargo twisted away, to deny her the pleasure. In the same movement he brought out the compact and placed it on her navel. She scooped it up and snapped the lid open and looked at her reflection in the little mirror. Glancing up at him, she muttered, "Some gift. Half the face powder is missing. Where did you come by it?"

"Off a dead whore, down Mexico way."

"You men . . ." She smiled. "Let you out of our sight for one minute and you're on another woman. Anything else in the pocket?"

"No. She wore a silver necklace and waist chain . . . and she carried a bullwhip. But I didn't relieve her of them."

"My word. A bullwhip? Really, Fargo, I didn't think you were into that sort of a thing. Was she good—in bed, I mean?"

"Wouldn't know—about the bed, I mean," he began. "Marie Mercier was a playful, adventuresome sort."

"I don't want to hear about your escapades with her." Candace snapped the lid shut. "But I will keep the compact. Marie had good taste in the facial powder she used—and her choice in men, I might add," she mocked. Ice-blue eyes watched him move to the wing-back to finish undressing.

He got in bed and lay on his right side to face her. She grasped his hard-on and stroked it slowly, mewing child-like, "Uhmm . . . nice, so nice."

He bent to her left nipple, to tease it with the tip of his tongue. During the movement, he glimpsed the tiny soft-brown areolae encircling it. He felt her body quiver as he tongued first one nipple erect, then the other.

Maintaining her slow but firm stroke, she murmured, "God, that feels good. The inside of my mouth is already getting dry."

Fargo knew what she meant; Miss Candy was feeling an orgasm starting to manifest. She arched her back, silently telling him to suck. He took in as much of the pillowy breast as his mouth could hold, and started sucking.

Her writhing body trembled as her hot breathing quickened. She was moaning, deep-throated now. "Oh, God . . . I'm exploding . . . inside. Suck, lover man, suck harder . . . please."

He felt her grip on his member, trying to stretch it to her hotness. Rolling onto her, she parted her legs, and he parted her short platinum hair. He felt her fingernails rake down his back as he thrust into the hot, moist opening.

Her knees raked his hips as she shoved up to take all of him, and she moaned, "I'm coming . . . I'm coming. God, but that feels good."

As she started bucking, he started thrusting with pistonlike strokes in a well-oiled but undersized cylinder. She gyrated in clockwise motions, he counterclockwise. She swayed her hips from left to right, he swayed right to left. He felt her heels dig into his hard butt as she whispered, "Faster, lover. Faster. Go deeper, too. Shove hard, all the way inside me. That's it . . . that's it . . . now you're doing it. Deeper, lover, go deeper . . . give it all to me."

He filled her sheath with a river of hot, throbbed spurts. As he did, her heels dug in tighter and she raised her hips to hold him inside, and started nibbling his nipples, kissing his chest.

Finally, her legs lowered onto the bed and she parted her silky thighs. They lay there bathed in perspiration and breathing hard while waiting for him to limber.

Miss Candy sighed, "Jesus, lover, you're still the best I ever had."

He found the strength to chuckle.

8

Fargo eased out of bed and moved without a sound to Miss Candy's window. Parting the curtains, he looked out on a dew-covered, early-morning scene. The river played among rocks that reminded him of bread dough ready for the oven. Beyond the shallow crossing stood the Conestogas—schooners of the plains—anchored in a peaceful blue lagoon of forget-me-nots. Both waited patiently for the sun to wipe away the dew.

An eagle and its mate patrolled low over the river. As Fargo watched, the female swooped to the water and snatched a trout from it with her black talons without interrupting her speedy, graceful arc of flight. She joined the male, which circled, providing her with protection. Then the pair of lifelong mates disappeared downstream, taking the meal to eaglets in their eyrie.

The sun crept over a snow-capped peak. Its rays kissed the snow and briefly smacked a spectacular rainbow of brilliant fire colors.

Yawning, Fargo released the curtains and stepped to the wing-back. After dressing quietly, so as to not awaken the shapely lump balled up, buried under the covers, he moved to the bed and gently got his Colt from beneath the pillow, then left the room.

Passing through the saloon, he met Henry the Eighth. The piano player's arms were laden with platters of breakfast food.

Fargo said, "Here, the Eighth, let me give you a hand with all those vittles."

"Just the coffeepot, Mr. Fargo." Henry Morgan smiled. "I got the rest balanced good."

Upstairs, Fargo rapped on the first door. Henry told

him, "No need to knock, Mr. Fargo. Just push Miss Roxanne's door open and go on in. She ain't up yet anyhow, but she soon will be."

Roxanne and a wrangler were facedown and naked on the bed. Fargo thought she had a fine-looking ass. Henry skillfully moved a platter from his left arm onto a small night table. He just as skillfully eased a cup off a finger. Fargo filled the cup. Morgan whispered, "Now, Mr. Fargo, hold it close to her nose so's she can get a whiff of it."

Fargo held the cup next to her nose, which twitched. Roxanne's dark eyes started opening slowly, then flew wide open when she saw Fargo, who shot her a smile and said, "Room service, ma'am. Coffee's ready." He touched the brim of his hat.

Henry Morgan chuckled as Fargo shut the door. They stepped to the door across the hall. "This is Miss Fifi's room," Henry said.

Fifi was awake and alone. She sat up and smiled when she saw Fargo.

"Ma'am, I'm pouring for the Eighth this morning," he said. "Do you want sugar and cream?"

Fifi shook her head.

They left.

At the next door, Morgan put a servile expression on his face and said, "Miss Wanda's meaner than a rattlesnake when she wakes up in the morning. Better watch out, Mr. Fargo."

They entered quietly. Wanda growled from beneath the covers, "Henry, if I've told you once, I've told you a thousand times to stop stomping on the floor when you come in."

"Yes'm, Miss Wanda."

"And stop calling me Miss Wanda. Plain old Wanda will do."

"Plain old Wanda," Fargo began, "where'll I set this coffee?"

Her head poked out of the covers. She rolled over and looked at Fargo. Wanda mellowed instantly. She asked, "Want some just woke up?"

Fargo shook his head. "Already had some." He poured a cupful and offered it to her. She shook her head and told him to put it on the bureau next to the platter. As they were leaving, Wanda hopped out of bed, put her back to them, started her morning exercise, bending at the waist and touching her toes. Fargo tipped his hat.

Melba, or Erin, was sound asleep. They didn't attempt to awaken her. The Eighth left her food on the bureau.

Fargo rapped gently on Annie's door and said, "It's Fargo, ma'am." He heard her leave the bed.

The door unlocked and she swung it open. Their eyes met, hers icy, his smiling. He held the coffeepot up. She stepped aside to let them in and drew the sash on her nightgown tighter.

"Morning, ma'am," the Eighth said cheerily. "Where you want me to put your breakfast?"

"On that little table. Didn't I see you playing the piano last night?"

"Yessum."

"You play well."

"Thank you, ma'am."

"Her name is Annie, Annie Hogg," Fargo told him.

"Pleased to meet you, Miss Annie." Henry smiled.

Moving a straight-back chair to the table, she said, "Don't compare me with Miss Candy. I'm in no way anything like her. Please call me Annie or Mistress Hogg." She sat to eat.

"Yessum, Mistress Hogg," Henry replied, stating his preference.

Fargo poured from the pot, saying, "His name is Henry Morgan. Most refer to him as the Eighth. Your choice, though."

"I prefer Henry, thank you," she answered.

Fargo gestured for him to leave.

"If you will excuse me, Mistress Hogg. I have other morning chores."

"You're excused," she said, slicing off a bite of fried ham.

When Henry was gone, Fargo closed the door and moved to look out the window.

He heard her say sarcastically, "Mr. Fargo, why do you linger in my bedchamber? To force yourself on me?"

"I wouldn't touch you if you were the last female on the planet," he muttered.

From his vantage point at the window, by looking down, he could see the flat roof on the bank and the open space between it and the saloon, including part of the space at the street. He glimpsed Ray and Frank Barrow as they walked past the scant opening at the street end. Something about the two bothered him, something out of place. Moving to the door, he said, "I'll be back."

And he heard her say, "I'll bet you will."

He went downstairs and outside in time to see the Barrow brothers riding east out of town. After watching until they were out of sight, he crossed the street and went to the stage office.

The ticket agent sat at his barren desk when Fargo entered. The man glanced up and said, "What can I do for you, mister?"

"When's the next stage due in?"

"Same time as I just told two men. Twelve o'clock today. Wanna buy a ticket? They didn't."

"No. I'm waiting for a passenger to arrive."

Fargo watched the agent pull open a drawer and bring out a sheet of paper. "If you will give me the passenger's name, I'll tell you whether or not he's on the stage. They telegraph the manifest up the line, as far as Creede."

"Her name is Tessa Hogg."

The agent looked. "Yep, she's on it, all right. Boarded in Pueblo."

Fargo thanked him, then went back to the saloon.

Miss Candy, her three saloon girls, and Erin were seated around a table, a whiskey bottle before them, when Fargo entered. He stepped to their table and said, "What are you women plotting?" He downed a slug of whiskey from the bottle.

They fastened their eyes on him, and Miss Candy replied, "Figuring out what to do with Erin—new wardrobe, hairdo, and all that."

"Major problem," Roxanne volunteered, "her being so shapeless and all."

Erin lowered her gaze and muttered, "I don't think I'm cut out for this line of work."

"Oh, I think you are," Miss Candy corrected. "My Methodist customers will adore you. Won't they, Fargo?"

He hesitated before he nodded. "Don't spend all your money, just in case everything doesn't work out for you." He touched the brim of his hat as he walked away.

Fargo met the Eighth in the hall. He was juggling the empty platters and cups, trying to keep them corralled, while he went to Annie's door. Fargo knocked on it and announced, "Fargo here."

The door was unlocked and opened. Annie still wore the nightgown. Henry hurried to the dishes and commenced trying to add them to the slippery stack. Fargo went over and helped him get everything balanced.

Henry said, "It's easier bringing them up than taking them down."

After he was gone, Fargo said, "The next stage is due at noon. Your cousin is on it."

"How do you know that?" she said.

"Because the agent showed me the list of passengers that he got from the telegraph office. I'm going to head out and meet it."

"Why would you do that?"

"I'm concerned about Tessa's safety."

"I'll bet you are."

"Look," he said disgustedly, "you're wearing my patience thin with that attitude. What happened to you, happened. I can't change that, and neither can you. All you can do is live with it and hope for better days. I'm that hope. So, stop grumbling and act civil toward me. I can't fight you and those out to kill you at the same time. Lock the door when I leave."

She sat on the bed, folded her arms across her bosom, and glared at him icily. He sighed and left.

Immediately upon riding out of town, he saw the Barrows' horses' fresh hoofprints, and dark, ominous clouds coming over the mountains. He nudged the Ovaro to gallop and matched the Barrows' gait. He rode until eleven-thirty, at which time he saw the same two sets of hoofprints coming from the opposite direction only to leave the road and head for high ground. He now knew that the Barrows had seen or heard him coming and had left the trail to evade him. He reined the Ovaro to a halt and looked up through the thickets and undergrowth to the rocky crest of the hill in time to see them top it. Fearing the worst, he put the Ovaro in a dead run to close on the stagecoach.

Rounding a bend in the road, he saw the stage had stopped. The men stood looking at a body lying on the ground under the coach. The left rear wheel had come off. He raced in, dismounting before the stallion completely halted, and asked, "Where is the female passenger?" He saw a man lying under the coach's rear axle, straining to push it up. The wheel lay broken on the ground. Two men held the spare upright.

A pinched-faced woman walked from behind the stagecoach and said haughtily, "She's gone."

An older man gripping a Bible added, "She left with two rough-looking men."

A third man added, "Riding double. They went that away." He pointed toward Wagon Wheel Gap.

The man trying to hold up the axle long enough for the others to put the spare in place, grunted, "She didn't seem to know them. Mister, you look strong. Can you give me a hand?"

"Come out from there," Fargo told him. "There's an easier way." A big tree limb lay on the ground nearby. He headed for it, motioning a man to come along.

Fargo raised the axle easily with the limb-lever. The man put the spare wheel on.

"I'm the driver, Claude Harris," the sweating man said. He extended his hand to Fargo.

Shaking the hand, Fargo asked, "Did the men hurt her?"

"Didn't look like it," the pinched-faced woman suggested.

"They walked her out of our earshot to talk to her," Claude said.

"Then she got in the saddle in front of the younger man," the Bible-holder said.

Fargo nodded and thanked them, then mounted up and headed for the Gap.

Within moments he rode into light, drizzling rain. Through it, he saw a woman sitting on a big rock beside the road. Fargo slowed the Ovaro to walk. As he came closer to her, she stood. She was about the same size and build of Annie Hogg, only her hair was midnight black. Even though covered from neck to ankles by a black dress, he could see she was shapely. A wide black patent-leather belt having a large silver buckle captured her waist, emphasizing her nice hipline. She wore a wide-brim ladies' hat, also black, held in place by a bright-yellow ribbon tied under her chin. Her face was prettier than Annie's, he decided, more feminine, due to the attention to the eyebrows and eyelashes, he supposed. The eyebrows arched perfectly; the long eyelashes curled nicely. Her lips were full with the upper being a perfect Cupid's bow. The corners turned up slightly, giving a hint of perpetual smile. He guessed her age would be eighteen. The young woman was picking bits of the undergrowth from her dress, a clear indication the Barrows had let her go in the green stuff.

He had to make sure. Tipping his hat, he asked, "You are Tessa Hogg?"

"Tessa Lovelace," she corrected. Her voice was husky.

"My mistake, ma'am. I understood Tessa Hogg was a passenger on this stagecoach. Must have been that sour-faced, older woman."

"No. Her name is Velma. She is Reverend Smythe's wife."

"Then . . . ?" Fargo looked at her questioningly.

"I'm she. I prefer Tessa Lovelace. Fits my personality better. Actually, I hate my real last name."

He held his hand for her to take and said, "Come on up. Sit in front."

She gripped his hand, hiked the hem of her dress, and kicked her right leg high. He yanked her onto the saddle. She immediately squiggled his crotch into the crack of her ass. He set the pinto to lope. The gait, and the absence of stirrups to use for leverage, caused her to jostle. The constant rubbing of her fanny on his member soon resulted in it swelling and stiffening. She obviously felt it, too, and looked over her shoulder and made eye contact with Fargo. He'd seen that same look in other females' eyes many times before. It promised, *I'm going to hold you between my thighs the first chance I get.*

He reckoned Tessa was more worldly than her cousin, Annie.

She asked, "What do I call you, cowboy?"

"I'm no cowboy, ma'am."

"You look like one," she quipped.

"Name's Skye Fargo. I also answer to the Trailsman."

"What does that mean?"

"One who blazes trails for others to follow later."

After a long moment of silence, she said, "I think I prefer your other name. Do you mind me calling you Skye?"

"If you wish, ma'am. I have no objections."

The drizzle suddenly changed to a hard rain. Already wet, they were now soaked to the skin. Their problem compounded when a lashing wind arose. The sky grew increasingly dark from the churning black clouds. Lightning flashed and cracked. Thunder boomed and rolled down the road. All of it combined to restrict Fargo's visibility. A flick of the reins put the pinto into a walk.

Tessa complained, "Can't you find a dry place to stop? I'm sopping wet."

"Me, too, ma'am. On the way to the stage, I spotted what appeared to be the entrance to a cave. I'm looking for it now."

"A cave? How exciting. Will you treat me like you're a caveman? Please say you will." Tessa pushed her buttocks against him firmly.

He ignored the movement—and her suggestion—and kept his eyes on the left side of the trail, waiting for a flash of lightning. A bolt struck a juniper nearby and exploded. During the brief garish brilliance, he saw the scant entrance halfway up the rocky slope. Others would have missed seeing it in broad daylight.

"There it is," he said.

"Thank goodness," she replied, and he heard her sigh heavily.

He angled the Ovaro left and went up the slope to the entrance. Tessa slid off the saddle and hurried inside. "Don't go in there," he cautioned, "till I have a look and tell you it's safe."

"Safe? What do you mean, Skye?"

"It might be a den of rattlesnakes."

As he dismounted, she pulled back to wait in the opening. He removed his saddlebags, Sharps, and bedroll and joined her. "Look in my saddlebags for matches. They're rolled up in buckskin."

She found them, struck one, and held it up. "Damn, this is sort of scary."

The ceiling towered out of the glow of the match. The floor was quite flat, except for the several tall stalagmites, he saw. He couldn't see either wall or the back because of the dimness of the tiny flame. But there were no snakes in the immediate area. Putting his bedroll and saddlebags on the floor, he said, 'I'll get some firewood." He handed her the Sharps. She watched him disappear in the downpour.

A few moments later he returned with an armload of firewood, pieces of dead limbs mostly, and his hands filled with dry leaves he found under a thick top layer of wet ones. He dropped the firewood upon entering the cave and took the leaves between two large stalagmites.

She watched him remove a small hatchet from the saddlebags and use it to split the wood. As he worked, he told her, "It's dry on the inside. I also found pitch pine. We'll soon have you a warm fire."

"Pitch pine? What's pitch pine?"

"A pine that got hit by a bolt of lightning. It's easy to start a fire with it. You'll see. The pitch pine is used to catch the other, slower-burning wood on fire. I brought the leaves to hurry things up."

She watched him arrange the wood over the leaves, then touched a match flame to them. The leaves flared. The pitch pine caught their flames. Just like he had said, the wood started blazing. He stood and watched the smoke be caught in an updraft. He told her, "We can't see it, but there is an opening up there, somewhere."

When he started to leave the cave, she asked, "Where are you going? Don't leave me here alone."

"To get my saddle."

"Won't your horse get away?"

"No, ma'am. He won't go very far."

He ducked outside. Tessa heard him talking to the

Ovaro while he removed the saddle. In a minute he brought the saddle inside and placed it back of the fire, saying, "We're stuck here till this rain lets up. Might as well use the time to get some—"

"Some? Some what? Are you suggesting . . . ?" she purred.

Taking off his neckerchief and hat, he glanced at her. She was untying the chin strap and smiling at him wickedly. "I was about to say, rest," he told her.

"Are we going to act naughty?"

He watched her loosen her belt. Releasing his gun belt, he answered, "Honey, you've been naughty ever since I found you."

She chuckled. "I was naughty long before I set eyes on you." She removed her hat and put it on the pinnacle of a stalagmite.

"It will be dry and warm inside my bedroll," he assured. He pulled off his shirt and spread it near the fire.

Looking at his broad shoulders and muscled upper torso, she gasped, "Beautiful. So powerful." She turned her back to him, bent over, and took off her high button shoes.

As she bent over, her buttocks widened, and as she removed the shoes, she wiggled sensuously.

He commented, "You have a magnificent derriere." He started pulling off his boots.

"So I've been told." Unbuttoning her dress, she said, "I want to feel your hands on it."

"You will. Other places, too."

She stepped out of her dress and said, "I can hardly wait."

He pulled off his Levi's. A peak appeared on his undershorts. He watched her eyes widen before she pulled off her petticoat. His own widened briefly when he saw her quite large but youthful breasts. The milk-white mounds were mirror-twins. Big brownish-pink nipples protruded proudly from soft-brown areolae the size of silver dollars.

Fargo paused in the unveiling long enough to spread his bedroll near the fire. When he looked again, she had drawn her bloomers down an inch below her bushy black pubic hair. Smiling provocatively, she drew them down another inch.

He hooked his thumbs in the waistband of his shorts and pulled them down to the base of his manhood, revealing his pubic hair.

He watched her breathing quicken. A slight twitching started by her right eye. She bent over to draw her bloomers down to her ankles. Her heavy breasts hung low and swayed gently. She held the pose, waiting for him to make the next move.

Fargo put his back to her to draw his shorts down and off. Glancing over his shoulder, he saw she had held the sensual pose and turned her buttocks to him, exposing a big fluff of black pubic hair in her crotch.

On the right cheek of her otherwise unblemished rump were several black moles. He thought it odd that the moles were confined to that cheek only.

One of her middle fingers appeared on the fluff and started rubbing it. When she looked around her right hip to see if he was watching, he turned slowly to face her.

Tessa came up immediately, turned, and mewed, "I want that gorgeous thing. I want to taste it."

When he nodded, she dropped to her knees and fed the crown into her mouth. He felt her hot lips tighten and draw his foreskin below his throbbing summit. Tessa started sucking. His fingers entwined in her jet-black, long hair and set her head in motion, going from right to left, while encouraging her to take in more and more.

The black-haired beauty was halfway down it when she started moaning her pleasure. "Uhmmm . . . aah . . . oh . . ." Her hands gripped his hard buttocks and pulled him to her face, forcing the joyous mating.

He felt her face bury in his equally black pubic hair. Fargo was amazed that she had captured him fully. Her lips encircled the base of his staff, tightened, and started coming up slowly. He heard her lips smack when they left his pinnacle.

Smiling, she looked up into his lake-blue eyes and whispered, "That was exciting for me. Thrilling. You?"

"I was pleasantly surprised," he admitted.

He lifted her to stand. She put her back to him and

pressed hard. Rubbing her fanny on his hard-on, she took his hands and pressed them to her breasts, then reached up and curled a hand around his neck. Her fingers squeezing on his neck signaled that his on her breasts gave her the most pleasure. When he pulled on them, the fingers squeezed extra hard and she groaned, "That's it . . . that's it . . . pull and squeeze, Skye, darling." Tessa pressed her head against his powerful chest and moaned her joy.

Fargo continued to massage and caress the two pillowy mounds for a while longer, then he cradled her in his strong arms and lay her on the bedroll. Tessa's hand clung around his neck. She pulled his lips to hers and invited him to kiss her openmouthed. He accepted the encouragement and lay atop her soft body to do it. He found the young woman did know how to kiss. Her hot tongue circled his once, then caressed the inside of his mouth and tongue.

She murmured hotly, passionately, "Oh, but this feels good to me. You taste so sweet, Skye, darling. I could kiss you forever and ever."

Fargo broke the kiss and moved down to her left breast and kissed it, then the right, before burying his mouth and nose in the soft, silky flesh. When he nibbled on the nipple, her hands went to his head, pulled down, and she moaned, "Jesus, you're setting me on fire. Yes, yes . . . that's it . . . suck harder. Don't quit."

He slid to the left breast. Squeezing it produced a firm bulge. He sucked in a mouthful and teased the nipple with his tongue.

Tessa's back arched and she gasped, "Oh . . . oh . . . oh . . . yes, yes, yes. My mouth . . . it's getting dry."

He felt her shudder. When it passed, he moved down and kissed her smooth, slightly rounded abdomen, not forgetting to probe her indented navel with his tongue. He felt her quiver as she writhed in anticipation of what was to come. Fargo didn't let her down. As she opened her thighs, he raised her hips. His tongue slid through the raven bush to her begging slit, which his tongue caressed before plunging between her blood-swollen lower lips and into her hot, moist love-nest.

That's when Tessa Hogg/Lovelace screamed, "Don't stop. That feels wonderful. Go high, darling. To the top of it." When he did as she had asked, Tessa gasped loudly, "I'm having a beautiful orgasm . . . Aagh! So good . . . so damn good." Her fingernails dug into his nape.

He waited for her to stop trembling, then moved up and positioned his blood-swollen organ for penetration into the slickened opening.

Her hands gripped his buttocks as she parted her legs wider and raised her hips. He entered slowly about halfway. She whispered, "Go deeper . . . oh, yes, go deeper. All the way." She pushed up to force him in.

Fargo thrust deeply and started rotating his hips.

Tessa matched his rhythm and gasped between clinched teeth, "Aagh . . . aagh! Oh, my God . . . I'm in heaven. Faster, Skye . . . go faster, and deeper . . . please, please, go faster." She started bucking and gyrating wildly. Her legs came up. He felt her heels dig into his buttock cheeks.

He erupted just as he heard the stagecoach pass by, Claude slapping his reins on his team's backs and shouting for them to go faster.

Tessa kept her grip on Fargo as she milked him dry. Only then did she release him and fall limp, her chest rising and falling with each exhausted breath she took. Limbering, he kissed her tenderly. He withdrew, rolled off her, and lay on his side.

Breathlessly, she whispered, "Caveman, I adore you. You're the absolute best I've ever had. Much better than all the young men who've had me. They don't satisfy me. You do. I had four, no, five orgasms."

He touched a finger to her lips to hush her and said, "Now, you are going to tell me where you were going with the Barrow brothers. I thought they would shoot on sight."

She didn't answer right away. Finally she asked, "That was their name?"

He nodded.

Tessa explained, "They told me my cousin was bad sick, maybe dying, that they came to meet the stage and speed me to her. So I went with them. Then they heard you coming, left the trail, and went up a slope. The man I was riding double with pushed me off the saddle into all those weeds. There was nothing for me to do except start walking back to the stagecoach. You know the rest."

Her story is plausible, he reasoned, but said, "Annie isn't sick, certainly not dying. The Barrows have tried to kill her several times."

Tessa gasped, "Kill her? My gosh, why?"

"I don't know exactly why, although I suspect they don't want her to go to the mine."

"Rainbow's End? Annie told you about it? If she did, she wasn't supposed to. Our fathers—"

"Both dead," Fargo interrupted. Watching her face, he was prepared to restrain her if needed. But it wasn't necessary. Contrary to what he expected, she took the revelation exceedingly well, not even batting an eye.

He reckoned she was in a state of shock until she calmly asked, "How—when did it happen?"

Fargo proceeded to recount where he found them and under what circumstances. She listened patiently as he told of the Apache capturing her young cousin and the other females, his and McCord's finding them in Diablo Canyon, and Vásquez's one attempt on taking Annie's life.

With the conclusion of his accounting, she rolled onto her stomach and asked, "Are you going to take us to the mine?"

"Perhaps. Annie said she wanted to talk to you about it first." He glanced at the moles, then ran a finger over one.

"Stop that." She giggled. "It tickles."

He propped on one elbow to see the moles better.

As he inspected them closer, she said, "I don't know what she wants to talk to me about. Neither of us knows the exact location of Rainbow's End. Did Uncle Roscoe tell you before he died?"

"No," he muttered absentmindedly. Now he saw they weren't moles at all, but tattoos. His memory rolled back to the specks of mud he'd seen on Annie's rump. "What gives with the tattoos?" he mused aloud.

Looking over her shoulder at him, she asked, "Didn't Annie tell you about them, show you hers?"

"No. You want to explain?"

He watched her roll onto her left side and draw her left knee to her waist, raising the right hip. Twisting to look, she reached over, pulled the right cheek up, and said, "When our fathers returned home, they had a crudely drawn map with them. It was in a terrible condition from so much handling. They wanted a secret map, one that nobody could steal, one that, if they did, they couldn't decipher. They made two maps and had them tattooed on our butts. A sailor did the work for free, just to get an eyeful of our asses.

"Anyhow, the part of the map on Annie's pretty ass shows where you have to be in order to locate the mine. It gets you in the right place to find Rainbow's End. The part on my right cheek gives the specific directions after you get there. So, you need the two pieces of the map in order to find the mine. Clever, huh?"

Fargo stared at the arrangement of the tattoos. "Damn clever. It's so much Greek without identifying words. It tells me nothing."

"That's where Annie and I come in," she began. "Our fathers had us memorize the verbal instructions."

Fargo toyed with his beard as he looked at her and remarked, "Seems to me like they went to a lot of unnecessary trouble in doing all this to you young ladies. Marking you for life."

"Oh, no, Skye, darling. They were protecting our best interests."

"That's what they said?"

"Uh, huh."

"What are the verbal instructions?"

Suddenly Tessa wasn't so sprite. She muttered, "I was afraid you would ask."

"You don't remember."

She shook her head. He laughed. . . .

9

The lovely young woman wanted to make love again. Fargo accommodated her. Five minutes into it, the deluge changed abruptly to a steady drizzle. The wind abated. By the time they were through, the sun had come out. Fargo went to the entrance and looked outside. "Come see this, Tessa," he told her.

"What?" she asked.

"Hurry."

She came and cuddled in his arms and they looked at bright, beautiful twin rainbows in the northwest. She whispered, "At the end of one of them is a pot of gold. Do you believe that, Skye, darling?"

He chuckled. "I stood on the top of a mountain once. A very high mountain, I might add. Down below was a broad valley. The sun was peeking over my shoulder. Rain clouds came over the mountain range in the far side of the valley. The down-draft was such that a thin mist filled the valley. A large, circular rainbow appeared in the mist." Changing the subject, he added, "We must be going."

Tessa drew his arms around her waist. "So soon? I could stay here with you forever. Why don't we linger a while longer?"

"No," he said. "We better get back and check on Annie. I left her in an upstairs room at the saloon."

Tessa turned in his arms. Looking up into his eyes, she said, "A bordello? How exciting. Knowing sweet Annie, she's behind locked doors with her legs crossed."

He tilted his face and kissed Tessa, then repeated, "We must go to see about her."

Reluctantly, she released him and moved to the fire.

They got dressed in the damp clothes just as slowly as they had taken them off. Fargo rolled up his bedding and tied it, then draped his saddlebags over a shoulder, picked up his saddle, and went outside.

Tessa came right behind him. "See, I told you your horse would wander off." The Ovaro was nowhere in sight. "We're stuck here for the night," she added hopefully.

Fargo whistled. The Ovaro knickered and trotted down the slope with his ears peaked. Still wet, the pinto's jet-black fore- and hind-quarters and white midsection glistened in the sunlight.

Tessa watched Fargo make the powerful stallion ready for the trail, and commented, "Your horse is magnificent, Skye."

"Yes, ma'am. He's the best. Raised him from a colt." He swung up into the saddle and put his hand down for her to take.

Moments later they headed for Wagon Wheel Gap. They rode in silence, Tessa drowsily, content to rest her back on his muscled chest, Fargo wondering if he could solve the apparent enigma on her butt. Maybe Annie can shed some light on the riddle, he told himself.

Arriving on the outskirts of the town, they saw people running, taking cover in doorways, diving to safety behind barrels and water troughs. Fargo heard no gunfire, but he did hear the explosion that shook the town, and saw the front of the bank be blown apart. Smoke from the blast instantly billowed out of the newly created opening.

His first concern was for Annie. He dug his heels into the Ovaro's flanks. The horse sprang forward in a full-out run. He reined to a halt in front of the saloon, coming off the saddle with his Colt drawn, before the stallion stopped skidding. He ran inside the saloon and shouted to Herbie, "Annie? Is she all right?"

The Eighth answered, "She's with Miss Candy."

Fargo passed Tessa on his way to the rear of the bank. He ran through the space between it and the saloon. Coming to the back end, he dived out and rolled to face four armed men standing near six horses.

Two men swung six-guns and fired at him. Their bullets whipped above him.

He shot both gunmen in the chests.

One catapulted into the side of a horse, the other spun around from the impact of Fargo's bullet.

The other two ducked under skittish horses' bellies. One hollered, "Chance! Blevins! You all get out here. Me and Chilli need help."

Fargo rolled away as Chilli opened fire. Slugs sizzled in the mud six inches from his head. Fargo shot Chilli in the head as Chance and Blevins came through the doorway. Both held bulging canvas bags in one hand, Smith & Wesson army issues in the other.

After glancing at Fargo, they commenced firing at him. Fargo leapfrogged just in time to hear the slugs spatter in the mud behind him. Coming to his feet, he crouched to take them on. But their horses were already running with the robbers hanging on the blind sides. Fargo tracked with his Colt, waiting for one of them to look over his saddle, but none did until after they were out of range. While reloading, he watched them climb into their saddles, hold the bags over their backs, and head northwest.

Fargo holstered the Colt and stepped inside the smoke-filled bank. A man lay sprawled facedown and groaning on the floor. Fargo rolled him over gently only to see the man was his old friend, Nicholas A. Theodore. "How bad are you hurt, Theo? It's me, Skye Fargo."

Theodore's eyes fluttered open. He groaned, "They knocked me in the head. Hurts like hell, but I guess I'm okay." He glanced at the walk-in safe and saw the massive door was missing, smoke still spilling out from below the upper part of what remained. Theodore asked, "Did they . . . ?"

Nodding, Fargo answered, "Yes. They made off with two full bags. There were six of them. I left three dead in the mud out back. Sorry I couldn't get the others." He helped Theodore stand on wobbly legs.

"I was just closing for the day when they broke down the back door and knocked me unconscious."

"You are lucky they didn't kill you. Did you sell your bank in Walsenburg?"

Walking into the safe, Theodore answered, "No, I still have it. I bought this one only two days ago. Look at this mess, will you?"

Fargo stepped into the opening. Theodore was clearing the smoke with his hands. Fargo asked, "Any idea of how much they got?"

"Not all of it, but enough," Theodore began. "I see they missed the larger denominations. The bastards grabbed only the smaller bills."

"Maybe I arrived in time."

"Maybe you did. Fargo, I know you won't accept a monetary reward, but I'll buy you a bottle of bourbon over at the saloon as a token of my gratitude for what you've done for the bank."

"And I will accept the bourbon."

"I will meet you in the saloon after I take care of things here." Theodore extended his hand for Fargo to take.

Shaking his hand, Fargo said, "You sure you don't need any help?"

"No, I'll bag up what's left and hide it in the oven of my kitchen stove."

"Be sure the fire's out." Fargo chuckled as he walked out the splintered front door.

Outside he saw the sheriff and his deputy were already putting together a posse to go after the bank robbers. He told them, "The robbers headed northwest. You will find three of them facedown out back."

The deputy's expression conveyed surprise as he said, "Three? You killed three of the Baxter gang?"

"Er, how do you know it was the Baxter gang? I thought the Baxters marauded towns over in Kansas."

The sheriff answered, "They rode in earlier, during the height of the storm. They went to the saloon first. Miss Candy recognized them. She sent the Eighth to tell me. But the storm caught me and Justin while we were out at Jim Metcalf's place, checking on a problem he has with wolves. They went northwest, huh?"

"Yes," Fargo answered.

"Well, they won't go far. That's rough country."

As Fargo headed for the saloon, he heard the sheriff

say to the posse, "All right, you men, hold up your rifles so's I can see them."

Fargo stepped to the swinging doors and paused to scan the customers' faces, to maybe spot the Barrow brothers.

Herbie noticed him, "Come on in, Fargo."

"Later, Herbie." He looked around for Tessa. "Herb, did a young lady come in here?"

"Miss Tessa Lovelace? She's in Annie's room."

Fargo pushed through the double doors and ordered a shot of bourbon. Wilson watched him toss it down. "Pour another, Herbie. Two drifters wearing dusters been here this afternoon?"

"Yeah, they were here. Walked in during the rainstorm. Drenched to the skin. Bought two whiskies each, then went back out into it."

"See where they went?"

Wilson shook his head. "They knew Annie was here, though. Asked about her. I told them we didn't have a saloon girl by that name."

Fargo left fifty cents on the bar and went outside. After looking up and down the street to maybe spot the duo, he went to the barber shop. The barber stood looking out the front window. As Fargo entered, the man greeted him, " 'Afternoon, mister. Beard trim and haircut?"

"No, thank you."

"Bath, then?"

"Yes, I could use one."

Fargo followed him out back and watched while the barber stoked the coals under a big cast-iron kettle. Fargo asked, "What's your name?"

"Buster. Buster Hix."

Fargo watched Buster start transporting buckets of cold water from a vat to a wooden tub. Pulling off his boots, Fargo said, "Two men came in your shop yesterday afternoon."

"Are you talking about the two no-good drifters who knocked me out?"

Nodding, Fargo asked, "Did you happen to see them today?"

"They rode by when it was storming, pouring down rain. After they disappeared in it, I went to fetch the sheriff, but Warner wasn't interested in chasing them down in all that rain. Said he'd look into the matter later."

"Oh, did he, now?" Fargo realized the Gap had a crooked sheriff on its hands. He asked, "Which way did the two men go in the rain?"

"Toward Creede. Anything else before I leave?"

Fargo shook his head. He poured four buckets of hot water in with the cold and got in the tub. While soaking with his eyes closed, he heard Miss Candy's voice say, "Lover, get out of that tub this instant." Opening them, he saw she spoke from the back door of the barber shop. "If you want a bath, I'll give you one," she offered caustically.

"Well, er, uh," Fargo stammered.

Miss Candy came and held open a towel for him to dry off with. Getting out of the tub, she wrapped him in the towel and said, "In case you don't know, I have one of those fancy brass tubs."

"No, I didn't know," he muttered.

"Well, I do. Ordered it from New York. Got it in the spring. I'll have Fifi fill it for us."

Us? he thought, pulling on his Levi's. It would have to be a damn big tub to hold the two of us.

Miss Candy was saying, "I'll go get things ready."

He watched her depart, then pulled his shirt on. Passing through the barber shop, he flipped a nickel to Buster and shot him a wink. As he went outside, he heard Buster mumble, "I wish I had her brass tub."

Fargo saw the Ovaro standing across the street, waiting in front of the café. The Trailsman walked over to the horse. Fargo looked inside the café windows and saw the four women and the children seated at a table. He stepped inside.

All the females wore new dresses and had their hair fixed. Touching the brim of his hat, he smiled and said, " 'Evening, ladies. I didn't recognize you at first. All of you look lovely, a far cry from when first I saw you in Diablo Canyon."

"Yes." Helga smiled. "Hot water and new clothes work wonders on women. Don't Henrietta and Martha look nice?" The two young girls blushed.

He said, "Yes. All of you look nice." Fargo caught himself in time to avoid adding, Considering all the hell you've been through.

Inez volunteered cheerily, "Ruth and I found work. She at the general store, and I as a maid in the hotel."

Fargo looked questioningly at Eva, who said, "The schoolmarm and I are talking about me assisting her, so I can be close to Martha when school takes up again after summer vacation."

"That's good." Fargo touched the brim of his hat again, saying, "If you lovely ladies will excuse me, I have urgent business to tend to. I hate to keep a lady waiting."

"Annie Hogg?" Helga inquired, showing a hint of a naughty grin.

"No." Fargo chuckled. "Annie still hates me."

"That girl," Helga lamented. "For the life of me, I don't know why she treats you like she does . . . after all you've done for her—for us."

Henrietta muttered, "I think she loves you deep down."

During the silence the youngster's remark produced, Fargo took his leave. Outside, he walked the Ovaro to the hitching rail in front of Miss Candy's Saloon and loose-reined him. Inside the saloon, Herbie Wilson handed him a shot of bourbon as Fargo passed down the bar. He set the empty shot glass on the far end of the bar and went to Miss Candy's door and rapped on it.

"Come on in, lover," he heard her say.

Swinging the door open, he saw she was already nude. He heard Fifi splashing water in an adjoining room. Miss Candy stepped over to him and stretched on tiptoes to kiss him. He took her by the waist and raised her begging lips to his. They kissed all the way into the bathroom. Opening one eye, he saw Fifi was nude also, kneeling next to the biggest brass tub he'd ever seen.

Fifi smiled up at him and said, "Water's getting cool."

Miss Candy whispered, "We'll set it to boiling, won't we, big lover?"

Fargo broke the kiss by lowering her to the floor. He

waited for Fifi to leave the room. Miss Candy saw his concern and said, "Undress, lover, and hop in the tub. Fifi will scrub our backs while we scrub our fronts."

The two women proceeded to undress him. He sat on the rim of the tub to pull off his boots. Miss Candy knocked his hand away, commenting, "We'll do it. You take the right, Fifi."

The women straddled his legs and bent to the task.

The boots came off. They stood and finished taking his clothes off.

Fargo stepped into the tub. Miss Candy followed and sat facing him. Fifi soaped a cloth and started scrubbing Fargo's back while Miss Candy cleaned his feet and legs. Finishing with his back, Fifi washed his shoulders and chest. Miss Candy warned her, "Don't work any lower. I'll get the rest."

Fifi moved and bent Miss Candy over and started scrubbing her back. Fargo felt Miss Candy's hands slide up his thighs and begin to gently massage him.

Miss Candy said, "Fargo, you're tough, tougher than rawhide. On the other hand, you can be gentle as a newborn. Those traits make you a big man." He felt her grasp tighten, then move up.

Fifi reached around and began washing Miss Candy's cantaloupe-sized breasts. Miss Candy pulled her into the tub, saying, "Show's over, lover. Now the three of us will get down to work."

They quickly moved from the tub to the bed, where they completely exhausted Fargo. Sandwiched facedown between the two energetic whores, he grunted, "Best damn bath I ever had."

Fifi left the bed, dressed, and blew him a kiss on her way out.

Miss Candy whispered, "What are you going to do with Annie and her cousin?"

"I don't yet know," he confessed.

Fargo and Miss Candy dressed, then went into the saloon. Before leaving her room, he glanced at her clock and noted the hour of the evening, nine o'clock. He saw Theodore standing at the bar and pulled him and Miss Candy aside, to a table where they could talk.

"I owe you a bottle of bourbon," Theodore said.

"Bourbon's on me," Miss Candy replied. "All he wants." She called to Herbie to bring a bottle of bourbon and three glasses.

Fargo said, "I think your sheriff and deputy were in cahoots with the bank robbers." He asked Miss Candy to summon Henry Morgan.

Henry and Herbie arrived at the same time.

Fargo said, "Herb, you might sit in on this too." The Trailsman repeated his opening statement, then went on to say, "Henry, when Miss Candy sent you to tell the sheriff the Baxter gang was in the saloon, did you find him?"

"Sure did."

"What did he say?"

"He said he would check on them. He asked if they were causing any trouble at the saloon. I told Sheriff Warren, no. Justin asked, 'Then what's the problem?' Sheriff Warren just looked at me and grinned. Did I do something wrong?"

"No," Miss Candy answered. "Continue, Fargo."

Looking at Herbie, Fargo said, "You told me the two drifters were here during the rainstorm."

"That's right," Wilson agreed.

Fargo said, "The barber, Buster Hix, said he saw them riding, heading for Creede. Buster told me they were the same two who knocked him out yesterday, then tried to dry-gulch Annie. So he knew their faces. He went to the sheriff's office immediately and reported they were riding out of town. Warren wasn't interested in going after them in the rain. When I told Warren and the posse which direction the robbers went, he said he and Justin had been caught by the storm while at Jim Metcalf's place, whoever he is."

"He told you a lie, Mr. Fargo," Henry said.

Fargo said, "Now, I want to be fair and not cast doubt on your sheriff, so I think we need Buster at this table."

Theodore volunteered to go get him. Pushing back from the table, he said, "Don't say another word till I get back."

They drank in silence while waiting. Shortly, Theodore

and Buster came through the double doors and hurried to join them. Buster asked, "What do you want me to tell other than what you already know?"

Fargo said, "Timing is critical. How long was it between the time you went to Sheriff Warren and when it stopped raining?"

"About five minutes. It stopped as fast as it had started."

"And you, Henry?" Fargo glanced at the pianist.

"Much longer than that," Henry answered. "I'd say an hour or better."

Miss Candy spoke next. "Rotten, no-good bastards! I knew I should have listened to my intuition. I pegged those two lawmen as being bad men the first time I laid eyes on them."

"How far is it to Jim Metcalf's place?" Fargo asked.

Miss Candy answered, "Jim's shack is about ten miles from town, in rough country."

Fargo had his answers. There was no possible way Warren and Justin could cover that much of that kind of real estate in five minutes.

Theodore asked, "Fargo, what are you thinking?"

"I'm thinking you will never see those two badges again. I'm thinking they will lead the posse on a wild-goose chase, then give it the slip and go straight to what's left of the Baxter gang. How much of your money did they get away with?"

"More than I first figured. Six thousand, five hundred and eighty dollars, to be exact," the banker sighed.

"Can you cover that much of a loss?" Fargo asked.

"Do you need a fast interim loan?" Miss Candy added solemn-faced.

"No loan necessary, thank you. I can protect the citizens' money by transferring the amount from my bank in Walsenburg."

Pushing back from the table, Fargo said, "Now that this mystery is taken care of, if you will excuse me, I have another riddle to solve."

They watched him go up the stairs. At Annie's door, he knocked twice, saying, "Fargo, here."

Tessa smiled as she unlocked and opened it. She wore her petticoat only. Annie was sitting on the bed, dressed in her nightgown. Tessa said, "We've been talking about you, Skye. Were your ears burning?"

Moving to stand at the window, he asked, "What else did you discuss?"

Annie answered, "She told me you saw her tattoo and questioned her about it. Mr. Fargo, you've not seen mine. Neither did I tell you anything about it. And furthermore, I won't show it to you, or discuss it."

The only thing that prevented his abandoning the two young cousins was his promise to the old man. Annie was severely testing Fargo's patience, pushing him to his limits. Grim-jawed, he strode to the door. He yanked it open and started to leave. With his back to them he paused and said, "I'll come for both of you in the midmorning. Be ready to travel. We're riding to Rainbow's End." He left the door open intentionally. Striding down the hall, he wondered how long they would talk about his last remark.

At the bar Fargo wedged himself between two young, rawboned wranglers. Miss Candy automatically half-filled a glass of bourbon and slid it across the bar to him. After drinking from it, he looked at her and said, "Candace, do you know what I'm ready to believe silly young females are good for?"

She touched his hand. "Screwing. What else?"

"That too, but I was about to say, playing games. Deadly ones."

Miss Candy slid her gaze to the top of the stairs. As she did, four men from the posse entered and leaned on the far end of the bar.

A townsman sitting at the poker table with Theodore and two other men shouted over the Eighth's music to the foursome. "Hey, Horace, did the posse catch the robbers?"

A hush filled the saloon as everybody waited for Horace to answer. "No," he finally said. "We lost them. Sheriff Warren sent us back. He and Justin are still out there."

Fargo and Miss Candy exchanged thoughtful glances.

10

Fargo left the saloon and rode to the livery. Old man Jonas Record held a lantern to his face and was ready to blow it out when Fargo came through the wide opening. Temporarily blinded by the bright flame, Jonas lowered the lantern. Shielding his eyes, he barked, "Goddammit, what'cha mean coming in here at this hour of the night? Can't'cha see I'm closed for the day?"

Fargo nudged the Ovaro forward into the light. Record's eyes briefly widened as he tensed and took a step back, favoring his left leg. Fargo watched him lean to shine the light on the pinto. Jonas croaked, "But I'm always open to the Trailsman. That is you up there, ain't it?" He raised the lantern as high as he could.

The big man eased from the saddle and offered his hand to the old man. Like Angus McCord, Jonas Record knew the Colorado Territory better than the back of his hand. He had been here a long time. Unlike McCord, who was a trapper supreme, Record prospected for gold. That was before Record's run-in with the grizzly. McCord had killed the big bear. Shot it dead with his .52 Spencer while the bear had Jonas down on the ground, mauling him.

It had happened early one morning, when ground fog covered the creek and filled the canyon where Jonas had made camp. Jonas' two pack mules, Lady Sandra and Pittsburgh Tom—named for the woman Jonas loved and the man who butted in: Jonas had shot both dead—awakened him, hee-hawing loudly and stomping. He knew right off that nothing would make them act that way unless a bear was after them. Jonas reckoned it was just one of the black bears he'd seen downstream the day before.

Armed with a pistol only, he shot in the air to scare the bear away. Seconds later the grizzly rose above through the fog. Jonas emptied the pistol in the big bear's chest, "For all the good it did," he would later say.

The huge grizzly caught Jonas backpedaling and pulled him to the ground. That's when Jonas wrenched his left knee. "It hurt so bad that I felt nothing else that bear did to me," Jonas had told Fargo. "I heard a rifle roar three times. The grizzly collapsed on top of me. Dead, of course. I didn't know whose warm blood I felt, mine or the bear's. I was too weak to get out from under it. The next thing I knew it was off me. Angus McCord looked down at me and jested, 'Blink once if you're alive, Jonas, twice if you're dead.' Angus had pulled the grizzly off me. Angus McCord and I go way back. Our paths had crossed many times before, but I didn't know he was around that morning."

Jonas had prospected for two more years, until the pain in his knee became so unbearable that he was forced to quit. He settled in Wagon Wheel Gap and bought the livery for all the gold he'd found—two measly nuggets.

His grasp on Fargo's hand was firm. Shaking it, he said, "Glad to see you again, Fargo. Saw you ride by with six scrawny women yesterday afternoon. What brings you to the Gap?"

"Can you take my horse?"

"Wouldn't want to sell him, would you?"

"Jonas, everytime I've left him here, you've asked the same thing. The answer is still no."

"Can't blame a feller for trying. Yeah, I have an open stall. Come on, I'll show you the way."

Following Jonas and the lantern, Fargo said, "Sure do wish I had Angus in on this one."

"How is the big son of a bitch? Watch that puddle."

Fargo stepped over it in time. Jonas opened a stall door. Fargo answered, "He and Magee were blind-drunk last time I saw them. They were busy burning Beaver Pond to the ground." He started removing his bedroll and saddlebags.

Dancing a jig, Jonas slapped his leg and laughed, "Goddamn, McCord finally did it. He did it, he did it! I always reckoned he would." Calming, the old man poked a finger in Fargo's chest and said, "McCord, he came through here—what?—a few days ago, last week. He was headed back to Beaver Pond. Been in high country 'bout six months. Claimed he wanted to get away from all the bullshit happening at the Pond—"

Fargo interrupted to steal Jonas' punch line. "All Angus wanted was a little peace and tranquillity."

The old man shot him a hard look. "I was 'bout to say that. Anyways, me and him got to drinking in Miss Candy's place. Angus said the only way he could get 'peace and tranquillity' was to burn Beaver Pond up. I didn't think he actually would do it, though."

Fargo removed his saddle and sat it on top of one side of the stall, then asked, "You ever hear of Rainbow's End?"

"Rainbow's End?" Jonas mused aloud. "Don't reckon I have."

Removing the Ovaro's bridle, Fargo changed the subject. "Six men rode into town when it was storming."

"They stopped here," the old man hurried to say. "Sorry-looking lot, they was. I recognize bad men when I see 'em."

"They were the Baxter gang from Kansas. Robbed the bank. Did you talk with them?"

"Sure did. The biscuit-dough-faced one asked where he could find the sheriff."

"Did he mention him by name?"

Jonas nodded and lamented, "For the life of me, I don't know why the town's people keep voting Sheriff Warren in. Yes, the man called him by his name."

"Get a bucket of good oats, will you, Jonas, while I'm checking his hooves?" They continued talking as Jonas limped to a bag of oats. Fargo said, "I don't think they will get the chance to vote for him again."

"Oh? Why?"

"Warren and Justin left the posse. Sent it back, actually."

"Hunh," Jonas snorted. "Those two couldn't track a column of army troopers riding elephants."

"Oh? Why do you say that?"

Handing the bucket of oats to Fargo, Jonas replied, "That bank was robbed three times the last eighteen months. Nary a one of Sheriff Warren's posses caught the bastards."

Fargo instantly suspected somebody other than Warren was the mastermind. He made a mental note to ask Theodore the name of the previous owner. Coming out of the stall, Fargo asked, "Did you by any chance see the two drifters ride into town earlier this afternoon?"

"Yes. They looked like drowned rats. Same ones that had me take care of their horses two days ago. Came and got 'em yesterday morning, before the rain."

"Did you talk to them?"

"I asked where they were from and where they were headed. The older one said they was from someplace in Virginny. I forgot the name of the town."

"Lynchburg?" Fargo suggested.

"Now that you mention it, yes. How'd you know?"

"Lucky guess."

"The young one said they was prospectors. Gold prospectors. Hunh! I knowed that was a lie. They didn't have nary one pan or hand pick twix' 'em."

Fargo stepped to hay piled against the far wall. Gathering an armload, he told the old man, "I think they went to Rainbow's End."

Jonas snorted, "That makes twice you have said that name. Now, you're gonna have to satisfy my curiosity." He watched Fargo dump the hay in front of the stallion. Before closing the stall gate, the Trailsman told him about the massacre and his promise to Roscoe Hogg. He dug the buckskin pouch out of his pocket, opened it, and dumped the nuggets into Jonas' palm, saying, "They came from Rainbow's End. And before you ask, I don't know the location of the mine."

Jonas whistled softly as he fingered the nuggets. His eyes seemed to twinkle and shine when he muttered, "Jesus, Fargo, do you know how much these are worth?"

"No. Not really. But you're about to tell me."

"Shit, Fargo, I don't know. Don't keep up with the price anymore. But they'd bring a lot. Wish I had found them."

"Hogg implied there were plenty more in the mine."
Handing them back, Jonas shook his head.
Fargo returned the nuggets to the pouch, stuffed it into his pocket, and shut the gate. Picking up his Sharps, he suggested, "My guess is the Hogg brothers were headed for Creede, the end of the line for Conestogas. I say Creede because that was where the Barrows were going."
"Barrows?"
"The two drifters. I saw four Barrows in the saloon at Beaver Pond. They were with a fifth man."
"Shorter than me?" Jonas cut in. "Balding?"
Nodding, Fargo said, "Go on."
"I saw him in Miss Candy's. He was drinking with two mean-looking drifters wearing dusters."
"That's the same trio. When did you see them, and which way did they go when they left the Gap?"
Jonas scratched his head and answered, "Several days ago. I didn't see them leave town."
Walking to the entrance, Fargo decided the bank robbery and the man with the Barrows were unrelated. He agreed to buy Jonas his fill of whiskey at Miss Candy's. Jonas eagerly accepted and blew out the lantern.
As they entered the saloon, it was love at first sight; Jonas stopped and stared at Melba/Erin. She was standing with two men at the bar. Her hair was done up in ringlets and she wore a loose-fitting red dress. A red ribbon corralled her hair. And her face looked different with rouge on her cheeks, darkened eyebrows and eyelashes. A tiny black mole that hadn't been there before adorned her face near the left corner of her lips, which were now painted slightly red. In a word, Erin looked appealing. Fargo hardly recognized her.
He asked, "Jonas, are you Methodist?"
Not taking his eyes off Erin, Jonas muttered, "Back in Chicago my mama raised me as one. Why?"
"Come on. I'll introduce you to the chicken."
"Oh, no," Jonas mumbled. "I don't think that is such a good idea." Lowering his voice to a whisper, he confessed, "Fargo, I've been impotent ever since the grizzly."
"No, you're not. It's all in your mind. Come on. Let's go meet her."

Jonas tagged along behind Fargo, who looked at the two men and said, "Pardon me, gents, but I have something to say to the little lady in private." He took her arm and led her near the piano. Jonas shuffled along, following them.

Fargo said to Erin, "My, my, but you do look nice."

"Miss Candy and Roxanne are responsible." She smiled. Out of the corner of her mouth she added, "Ain't my new mole the prettiest thing you've ever seen?"

"The mole looks pretty," he said, pulling Jonas from behind him. "Melba—"

"Erin," she corrected.

"Er, uh, yes, Erin, I want you to meet my Methodist friend, Jonas Record. Jonas owns the livery down the street."

Erin bent and kissed Jonas' cheek. A wide smile that had to hurt Jonas froze on his battered face. "Damnation, you're the prettiest whore I ever laid two eyes on."

"Well, thank you, Jonas. I do believe you're the handsomest livery owner I've ever met. What say we go up to my room and get better acquainted?"

Jonas looked with begging eyes for Fargo to come to his rescue. Fargo just smiled as he walked away from the two. He heard Erin put to Jonas, "Don't be afraid. I won't bite . . . too hard."

Fargo crowded in beside Theodore at the bar. Miss Candy served Fargo a bourbon. He shot her a wink, then looked at the banker and asked, "Who did you buy the bank from?"

"A young woman. Edward Loch's widow. Her name is Marlena. Why?"

"How well did you know the Lochs?"

"I knew Ed from Denver. I'd say we went back five years. He was a good man, a conservative banker."

"Her?" Fargo downed his bourbon and held the shot glass out for more.

"The first time I saw Marlena was at their wedding in Denver. She was twenty and Ed fifty-five. He was a widower. Ed couldn't function without a woman around to take care of his needs. I didn't see her again till Ed died."

"When was that?"

"October fifty-eight. The next time I saw Marlena was at Ed's burial."

Fargo mentally counted the months since Loch had died.

The banker continued, "I didn't see Marlena again till she approached me and asked if I knew of anyone who might be interested in buying the bank."

"Did you know the bank had been robbed three times after Loch's death?"

Theodore visibly stiffened. He looked at Fargo and frowned when he said, "No. She didn't tell me that."

"Is Marlena Loch still around?"

"No. She left the same day the bank was robbed. Do you think—"

Fargo interrupted to say, "Yes, I think she had something to do with it." He motioned Miss Candy to come. As she filled the shot glass, he asked her, "Do you know anything about Marlena Loch, especially her morals?"

Miss Candy suggested, "The woman would have made a good whore. It's common knowledge in certain quarters that she was sleeping with Sheriff Warren on the sly. Both before and after Ed died."

Turning to the stunned banker, Fargo said, "Marlena set it up with Warren. They're out there now dividing the money."

Theodore ordered a bottle of whiskey and took it to a table and started drinking seriously.

Fargo moved to a table, too. He joined three men playing five-card draw, to pass time while waiting for the customers to thin. At midnight Miss Candy gave him the high sign that she was ready to go to bed. He played two more hands—lost both—and left the table.

In Miss Candy's apartment, she said, "You're restless as all hell." Then she asked, "When do you leave?

Undressing, he said, "In the morning."

"Do you know to where?" she asked from the bed.

Slipping beneath the covers with her, he answered, "To Creede. I don't know where after that. Maybe nowhere."

Hugging him close, she whispered, "Will you come back?"

"I don't know." He leaned over and blew out the lamp.

Somebody knocking on the door jarred Fargo's eyes open. His gun hand automatically brought his Colt from under his pillow. Tessa's tipsy voice spoke from behind the door. "Fargo, I need you to help me with Annie."

He was out of the bed instantly, moving quickly to the door. Miss Candy lit the lamp as he parted the door by a foot. Tessa stood there buck-naked, bracing herself against the hallway wall. He asked, "What's the problem?"

Tessa rolled away from the wall and slumped into his arms. In a soused voice she muttered, "Annie's in the saloon."

Fargo lowered her to the floor and glanced at the clock. The time was four-ten. While he pulled on his pants, Miss Candy got into her gown. She led the way with the lamp as he followed, carrying Tessa's limp body into the dark saloon.

Annie was sitting, slumped facedown over a poker table. She was nude also and reeked to high heaven of liquor. The banker lay on the floor by the piano. He snored softly. Fargo sat Tessa in the chair opposite Annie's. Miss Candy brought a wet rag and started wiping Tessa's face, shoulders, and neck.

Tessa stirred out of her stupor. Batting her eyes, she giggled. "I got Annie drunk so you could see our tattoos."

Fargo lifted Annie from the chair and laid her facedown on the table. Then he did the same with Tessa, whom he had to hold down to keep her from rolling off. He told Miss Candy to hold the lamp close to the pair of rumps so he could view the tattoos. He'd seen Tessa's eight molelike tattoos earlier. Annie's five were not all black. Two were blue and one was red. He had already heard Tessa say she had forgotten the verbal instructions that applied to her tattoo. Annie was in no condition to say anything, even if she would, which he doubted. Tessa had said Annie's fixed the mine's general location.

He concluded that the two blue dots on Annie's left

cheek represented bodies of water, the red mark the mine, and the two black dots high mountain peaks. Fargo racked his brain, searching for a two-lake, two-mountain arrangement that matched the tattoos, and failed.

"What do you think?" Miss Candy muttered.

"I think I need the services of somebody who knows this territory better than I do. Go see if Jonas Record is still in Erin's room."

"Jonas Record?" she echoed.

"Yes. He will know how to put together the pieces of this puzzle."

"I'll go check on him."

Fargo drank and continued to glance from cheek to cheek while she was gone. The more he studied the tattoos, the more they made no sense to him. Miss Candy coming down the stairs broke his thoughts.

She was grinning into the lamplight. She said, "He's in her room, all right. I found them buck-naked and wrapped in each other's arms, sound asleep. She awakened easily. They're coming down."

Jonas appeared on the top landing dressed in his red long johns. Erin followed, pulling a robe around her bony body. Both looked totally exhausted. Jonas came down the stairs shakily, Erin steadying him. At the table both collapsed into chairs. Fargo shoved drinks before them. Jonas grasped his glass with both hands and drank it dry. The old man's red-rimmed eyes focused on Fargo.

Jonas mumbled, "I'm tired. Why did you wake me?"

Fargo nodded to the two young women lying naked side by side on the table.

Jonas' gaze moved slowly onto them. He muttered, "Fargo, I don't have the strength left. But I thank you for the offer."

"No, Jonas. I want you to look at their asses," Fargo said.

"Their asses?" Jonas repeated in a stronger voice. He leaned over to look and said, "Fine pair of butts. So?" He held the glass out to Fargo for a refill.

Pouring, Fargo commented, "Look at them again. This time focus on the moles."

Jonas stood and moved between their legs to look.

Miss Candy held the lamp close to their fannies. Jonas bent, brought the tattoos on Annie's butt into focus, and mumbled, "Damn strange moles on this one's left cheek. Two look blue and one is red." Shifting his gaze to Tessa's rump, he said, "But these are normal."

Fargo explained, "They're all tattoos. They are maps, showing the location of Rainbow's End, a gold mine."

Jonas suddenly became wide awake and found a burst of energy. Cutting a sly grin Fargo's way, he said, "I did hear you correct? You said a gold mine?"

Nodding, Fargo added, "You heard right. It's somewhere in Colorado. My guess is in the high country northwest of here."

Not wanting to influence Jonas, Fargo waited to hear his assessment of the maps. Jonas bent again and scrutinized both arrangements. Rubbing his face, he said, "Never seen anything like it. Maps always have words. There ain't no words, Fargo. Neither do they give any indication of where the mine is located. Like a mountain or . . . Wait a minute. Those two blue spots could mean water. The two black ones below them . . . hmmmm. Mountain peaks?"

That was verification enough for Fargo. Jonas would never figure out Tessa's tattoos without his help. "Earlier, when we were in a cave, Tessa—she's the black-haired one—showed me her tattoos and—"

"Did she now," Miss Candy interrupted. Her eyes swept down Tessa's full length, then settled on Fargo's.

Fargo ignored her intrusion and continued, "She doesn't remember the verbal instructions, but she did tell me that the arrangement of tattoos on her ass are the markers that lead to the mine. Her cousin's tattoo shows where you have to be standing in order to find the general location of the mine. Problem is, Annie refuses to tell me her verbal instructions. I'm at a standstill. So, my hope was that you might recognize the landmarks on Annie's rump."

"Hold the light closer," Jonas told Miss Candy, "while I take a gander at 'em."

Fargo knew that during the silence Jonas was identifying all two bodies of water he could remember that were anywhere near two mountain peaks. Finally, Jonas shrugged and sighed, "Colorado is covered up with lakes and ponds, not to mention high mountain peaks. This would easily match fifty places. Fargo, I can't help you."

"Take another look at Tessa's."

As he looked, Jonas shook his head slowly. "Without words . . ."

Nodding, Fargo acknowledged, "I know, I know. Thanks anyhow, Jonas." He poured him another drink.

Jonas sat. He raised the glass to his lips, paused, and glanced at the two tattooed bottoms. "Mebbe if I had 'em to look at while I think on it—"

"Are you asking for pencil and paper?" Fargo asked.

"Yep." Jonas tilted the glass of whiskey and took a swallow.

"Behind the bar," Miss Candy said. "I'll get them."

She came back carrying a plain sheet of white paper and a stub of a pencil and handed both to Jonas. Jonas made outlines of their fannies, then penciled in the "moles." Looking at his handiwork, he muttered, "Like I done said, Fargo, I'll thunk on it. May come to me. I ain't promising nothing, though." Pushing back from the table, Jonas looked at Erin and nodded toward the stairs.

As they left, Fargo carried Tessa to bed first, then Annie. Upon his return, Miss Candy met him at the end of the bar. Pouring two shot glasses of bourbon, she allowed, "Lover, my sixth sense—call it a female's intuition—tells me you're heading into real trouble with those two."

Fargo took the drink to a front window. Sipping the bourbon, he stared thoughtfully at the lamp's reflection in a pane. An early-rising rooster crowed and broke his reverie. He turned and looked at Candace, nodded toward the hallway.

She met him in the opening and put her arm around his waist. Fargo had much to think about, but it would have to wait until dawn.

11

Fargo awakened well after the roosters ceased crowing. He nudged Miss Candy and told her three times that he wanted the big brass tub filled with bath water. Each time she snuggled deeper inside the bedcovers. Finally he got out of the bed and filled it himself . . . with ice-cold water. Settling down into the water, he shouted a war whoop that rattled the windowpanes.

When Miss Candy came within range, he pulled her into the tub. She gasped and sputtered, hollered and stiffened, and tried to get out. He pried her fingers off the rim of the tub and held her head and shoulders down in the water. She kicked and clawed, shivered and fumed, "Let me up, you big son of a bitch. I'm freezing to death. Goddamn you."

Chuckling, he let her go. Miss Candy fled to her warm spot in the bed. Fargo started soaping down, talking to her all the time. "I've figured out what happened. The four Barrow brothers and another man were in the saloon at Beaver Pond. Remember? You saw two of them and Baldy in your place. When they left, they headed straight to the mine. They're already there, working it. That means somebody other than Roscoe Hogg and his brother knew where to find the mine.

"Annie was supposed to die in the massacre. Vásquez and his boys were to see that she died. But after seeing how young and good-looking she was, they took her captive and planned on selling her as a love-slave. When Angus and I came along and saved her, Vásquez tried to take her life."

"Who in hell is Vásquez?" Miss Candy's muffled voice shouted.

Fargo explained, then continued, "I was a fly in the ointment, meaning the Barrows and the man with them heard me say that Vásquez took Annie captive and that I was going after them. So, in the event I succeeded, they left Frank and Ray Barrow behind to kill her.

"That means they presumed Tessa knew the way to Rainbow's End. But she didn't. I say Baldy was on that wagon train. Either Roscoe or Charlie told Baldy about the mine."

"Lover, this is interesting, but you're rambling, jumping from thought to thought," Miss Candy intoned.

"Hear me out," he said, getting out of the tub. "Frank and Ray had to intercept the stage to learn from Tessa the way to the mine. Before you ask, I'll tell you why they didn't know the way. Baldy didn't take the time to explain it to them. He took the fast and easy way out and simply told them to meet Tessa's stage in the Gap and tell her they were to escort her to Rainbow's End. Along the way she would tell them where to find it. At that time, they would kill her."

Fargo nudged the lump under the covers and said, "You listening?"

Her head poked out. She snapped, "Yes, go on."

"The Barrows probably deduced I was taking Annie to the mine. When they learned Tessa didn't know the way, they dumped her."

"Why didn't they kill her?"

"They planned to. That's where I came in. You see, they figure Annie showed me her tattoo and gave the verbal instructions. They didn't know it was a two-part map, Tessa having the other half. She told them, probably showed her ass, and said her memory failed her. Frank and Ray were lost at that point."

"Didn't you tell me you thought Tessa was in cahoots with the Barrows?"

"I've changed my mind about her being in on it. I now think she really doesn't know the mine's location. She's as lost as any of the rest of us."

"I think that's funny." Miss Candy chuckled. "The blind leading the blind."

"Yes. Back to your intuition. I agree that I'm walking

into real trouble with these young beauties. The moment Frank and Ray know they're close enough to Rainbow's End to find it, they'll try to dry-gulch all three of us."

Watching him dress, she said, "You be careful, hear me, big lover? I'd ride around Creede if I were you."

He shook his head, saying, "I want the Barrows. The only way to get them is to lead them to the mine."

"I repeat. You're walking straight into hell with your eyes wide open. Why?"

"I promised Roscoe Hogg." He bent and kissed her good-bye, then fetched his Sharps and saddlebags and left.

In the saloon the Eighth advised him that when he had brought the two young women's breakfasts, they were sound asleep. Fargo hurried up the stairs and knocked loudly on their door, yelling it was him. After what seemed an hour, Tessa unlocked it. She was already crawling back into the bed when he opened the door.

He went over and jerked the covers back and growled, "Get up and get dressed. Hurry. Meet me down in the saloon."

Tessa stared at him. "I'm sick," she said weakly.

"Get on your feet," he snarled. "We have things to do." Three strides put him in the doorway, where he paused to add, "You can be sick later."

Going down the hallway, he heard her mumble, "You insensitive bastard."

Fargo waved off the drink Herbie poured for him. "Got a cup of coffee back there?" he asked hopefully.

Herbie reached below the bar and brought out the coffeepot. Fargo was working on his fourth cup when he saw Tessa and Annie on the top landing. They looked terrible. Green-faced and moving slowly, as though walking on eggshells. He watched them wobble down the stairs and come to the bar. Both braced themselves on the lip of the bartop and stared glassy-eyed at it. Herbie poured and shoved two cups of coffee in front of them. All it took was a whiff of the steaming brew to send them flying out the swinging doors. Fargo followed with the two cups and watched both drape over the hitching rail to throw up.

Wiping her mouth with the back of her hand, Tessa choked out, "I'm dying."

"No you're not," he said. Offering her a cup, he added, "Drink it. You'll feel better."

She looked at him doubtfully, but did as he suggested. "My poor head is pounding. My stomach is churning. Fargo, I feel like shit."

Gagging, Annie turned and stared at him. He shot her a smile and a wink, then said, "Honey, last night I saw your tattoo."

"You bastard," she muttered, and turned and vomited again.

He handed the other cup to Tessa and gestured for her to give it to Annie after she was through. Annie refused the coffee. Fargo carried the cups inside the saloon and set them on the bar. Returning, he said, "Follow me, ladies. Time to buy you new clothes." He headed for the general store.

They followed slowly, clutching each other to prevent stumbling and falling in the dirt. In the store, he watched them enter and flatten their backs against the wall next to the door. Fargo told the man behind the counter, "Fix them up with new Levi's, shirts, and boots. Everything for the trail."

"Bedrolls and saddlebags, too?" the man inquired.

"That too. Fill my and their saddlebags with grub for the trail. Don't forget the coffee. I'll be back shortly to get them." Going outside, he said, "You two behave. Don't give the man any trouble."

Fargo went to the livery to get his horse. Jonas hadn't gotten there yet. That brought a grin to Fargo's face, for Jonas was a known early-riser. He backed the stallion out of the stall to curry him down. He was nearly finished when the old man staggered into the entrance. Fargo watched him grab one side of the opening and take a deep breath. Concerned, Fargo asked, "You all right, Jonas?"

The old man jumped as though shot. " 'Course I am," Jonas grunted. "What makes you think I'm not? I didn't think anybody was here. You should've made some noise, standing back there in the shadows."

Fargo chuckled. He'd caught Jonas being human, and the old man felt embarrassed. Erin had obviously cured his impotency . . . many times. Fargo set the dandy brush to work on the Ovaro's withers. He heard Jonas coming toward him slowly, dragging his feet.

Leaning on the stall gate, Jonas confessed, "Fargo, I ain't as young as I used to be. Time was when I could have made her holler uncle."

"Erin wear you out?"

"Four or five times. I'm sore as hell down there. Too sore to touch. I mean, it feels raw. You know, tender."

"No, Jonas, I don't know."

"Bullshit. She told me 'bout you and her screwing one night at the Pond. So don't tell me you ain't rode on her bones. You cain't get away from that thing. She wiggles it all over you. Shit, I'm sore."

"The fanny maps?"

Stretching, Jonas yawned, "Didn't get a chance to think on 'em yet. Too busy trying to hog-tie Erin. But I have the maps I drawed in my pocket."

Fargo handed him the dandy brush and started putting the saddle blanket on his horse. "Jonas, I need two sound horses. Got any for sale?"

The old man limped into heavy shadows at the rear of the mammoth barn. Fargo had the saddle on when Jonas came back leading a chestnut mare and a dun filly. "How's these?" Jonas asked. "I'll let you have 'em for fifteen dollars apiece."

Fargo paused to check their teeth. "Sold," he said. "Can you fix me up with saddles and tack for them?"

"Certainly," Jonas grunted. He disappeared back into the gloom.

Fargo had the bridle and reins in place by the time the old man returned, lugging the first saddle. Placing it to ride the top board on the gate, Jonas said, "That red mole on her ass could mean the mine. What do you think?"

"I agree."

Fargo went with him to get the other saddle. On the way, Jonas made another observation. "We both know there's beavers' ponds all over most of Colorado, especially in the places that me and most other men have prospected for gold."

Jonas was leading up to something. The old man was "thunking." Fargo said, "I agree. What are you thinking?"

Jonas pointed to the saddle. Gathering up the bridles, reins, and blankets, he answered, "I'm thunking if I made those maps I wouldn't make blue for no beaver's pond. Beavers' ponds come and go with the changing of the seasons. You know, here today, gone tomorrow. I'd make blue stand for water that I knowed was going to be around all the time. Like a lake."

They'd already decided as much. Jonas was simply getting around to identifying possibilities. Walking back to the stall, Fargo said, "Start on the far side of Creede, then fan out. I'm guessing the mine is close to Creede. Otherwise, the Hoggs would've taken another route and made arrangements to meet Tessa farther north."

Jonas sighed heavily, shook his head once, then said, "I found those two nuggets the afternoon before the morning the grizzly got me. I was 'bout halfway up Henson's Creek, working my way back to where the creek empties into the Gunnison River. Near a place called Gunsmoke Gulch. There are two lakes near there. San Cristóbal is the biggest. It's on the Gunnison. Upstream a short ways from Henson's Creek. The other is called Crystal Lake. It's small. High up in the mountains. You cain't see it till you're right up on it."

Encouraged, Fargo said, "I've seen those two lakes. And I know the creek. Go on, Jonas."

Draping the blankets over the horses' backs, Jonas continued, "Only thing wrong is . . ." He dug the map out of his pocket and showed it to Fargo. Drawing the big man's attention to what both had agreed were probably mountain landmarks, Jonas went on. "The problem is, these mountains are in the wrong place. On the map they're below the lakes, not above."

Fargo took the maps from him and turned the sheet upside down. "Is that better?" he asked.

Jonas considered them only briefly before saying, "Now the lakes are in the wrong places. If this mountain on the left is Red Cloud and the one on the right is Uncompahgre, then San Cristóbal has to be below and to the left of Crystal Lake, not above it and to the right. So, Fargo, anyway you look at it, I guess it was hopeful thinking on my part." He took the sheet of paper from Fargo, folded it, and tucked it in his hip pocket, saying, "Mebbe I made a mistake when I drawed it. I'd need to take another gander at that butt to be sure."

Fargo chuckled. "I don't see that happening."

"We could get her drunk again," the old man persisted.

"No, Jonas. Annie will open up and tell me the landmarks. I just have to make her comfortable with me. It'll all work out, I'm sure."

Nothing more was said between them until the two horses were saddled and bridles and reins put in place. Watching Fargo secure his bedroll to the Ovaro, Jonas mumbled, "Fargo, I love her." Assuming a fighting stance, the old man added, "We're friends, Fargo, but I'll fight you for her if you try to take her away from me."

Fargo looked at Jonas' balled fists. The old-timer is serious, he thought, but said, "No fight necessary, Jonas. You've killed one man over a woman. I don't want any part of your temper. Erin is yours. I won't mess with her any further. That's a promise." He extended his hand to Jonas.

Jonas was cautious in grasping it. Pumping it, he said, "I'll name our first boy after you." Jonas said it as though there was no doubt in his mind that he'd father several sons.

Fargo nodded. Jonas walked him as far as the entrance, where they waved good-bye. The Trailsman led the horse to the general store. The cousins were sitting in chairs on the porch.

Tessa pushed her new black cowboy hat back and said, "We thought you'd forgotten about us. What took you so long?"

For the time being he ignored her. After hitching the horses, he went inside.

The man said, "Your bill comes to twenty-two dollars and sixty cents." Touching the saddlebags, he added, "As you can tell, I've filled them with grub."

"Do you carry bourbon?"

"No. But I got whiskey and gin."

"Four pints of whiskey for me and one pint of gin for the ladies ought to be about right." Fargo intended to take another "gander" at Annie's fanny. He settled up with the clerk, then carried the saddlebags and liquor outside.

Stuffing the liquor in his bedroll, he told them, "We will leave the horses here and go to the café for breakfast."

Annie said, "If you're planning to get us drunk and take liberties with us, you have another think coming."

Fargo replied through an easy grin, "I wouldn't think of taking liberties with you. You're too cold for me. 'Icy' is a better word."

They watched him secure the saddlebags, then followed him to the café. On the way Tessa's husky voice purred, "Fargo, am I too icy for you?"

Grinning, he shook his head.

Annie snorted, "Tessa, I'd be pure ashamed of myself, talking like that, if I were you."

And he heard Tessa say, "Well, my sweet cousin, you're not me. I say what's on my mind. I'll be glad—no, eager—to take him off your hands every chance I get."

Fargo opened the café door for them. They sat at a table next to the front window. Fargo ordered three scrambled eggs, bacon, biscuits, and flapjacks. The women asked for one egg each and fried ham. The waitress poured coffee. After she left, Fargo said, "We're heading for Creede. We can expect trouble on the way."

Annie put her cup down. "From the men who tried to shoot me?"

He looked at her from over the rim of his cup and nodded. After taking a swallow, he told them, "I think I know the location of Rainbow's End."

That triggered a gasp from Tessa. "You do?" She glanced at Annie.

Annie was quick to say, "I didn't tell him. So quit looking at me like that." Annie's eyes darted to Fargo as she went on,

"You're lying, Mr. Fargo. Trying to cause me to make a slip of the tongue. It won't work, Mr. Fargo, it won't work. You don't have the vaguest idea where Rainbow's End is."

He leaned back and had his coffee. The food arrived. Munching on a strip of bacon, Fargo asked Annie, "Then why are you going with me?"

She glanced up at him, started to speak, and took a bite of egg instead.

Fargo waited.

Finally Annie said, "Because I'm more scared of those two men than I am of you."

"That doesn't make any sense," Tessa interjected.

Annie turned to her cousin. Sternly, she admonished, "Makes all the sense in the world. If I didn't go, then they'd learn about it and come back and shoot me. They might shoot me anyhow, even if I go. Mr. Fargo enjoys killing people. If they attack us, maybe Mr. Fargo and those two men will kill one another. That way we can go on to the mine and not have to worry about them showing up. I know the way to the mine." She poked a piece of ham in her mouth and looked at Fargo.

First he ate a flapjack, then said, "I agree. You've got it all figured out, haven't you, Annie?"

"That's correct," she answered in a cocksure tone.

He wanted, needed to shake her confidence, give her—both of them—a true enigma that would be mind-occupying. "Not quite," he said. "You're overlooking something."

"What?" Tessa asked.

He ignored her and kept on eating.

After a long silence, Annie spoke. "Tessa, he's playing with our minds. Trying to trick us. Don't fall for it."

Fargo detected a lack of conviction in Annie's words. She wasn't all that sure of what she said. He finished his cup of coffee and pushed back from the table. "See you at the horses," he said.

They watched him cross the street and enter Miss Candy's Saloon.

Herbie, the Eighth, and Roxanne were washing and polishing glasses. Miss Candy was sitting at a table with the other saloon girls. All four had cups of coffee before them. Standing at the table, Fargo looked at Erin and said, "Jonas was ready to whip my ass over you. What in the hell did you do to him?"

Erin muttered sheepishly, "Stirred his coals. He told me it wouldn't get hard anymore. I showed him different. I had fun doing it."

Miss Candy asked, "You three ready to head out?"

Fargo nodded. "Came to say good-bye."

Miss Candy rose and came to him. Curling an arm around his neck, she stood on tiptoe and kissed him passionately. "Take care, big man. You know my heart goes with you."

Nodding, he said, "I know, and I will." Scanning the saloon girls' upturned faces, he told them good-bye. On his way out, he stopped at the bar and shook hands with Morgan and Wilson and kissed Roxanne's cheek. There was nothing more to be said or done, so he left.

The cousins were walking to the horses. He intercepted them, saying, "It's a beautiful day, ladies."

Annie looked up at him and glowered. He saw her jaw muscles tighten, her lips draw thin.

Fargo grinned and continued, "A perfect day for killing somebody."

Ten minutes later they rode around a bend in the trail and lost sight of Wagon Wheel Gap.

At sundown Creede came into view. The small town sat on the edge of the frontier. Few souls ventured any farther than Creede. Those who did left their wagons behind, for the ruts ended here.

Fargo asked, "Ladies, have either of you been to Creede before?"

Both shook their head.

Tessa allowed, "Sounds like a lively little town, though. Exciting. My kind of place."

As she spoke, they heard gunfire. Seconds later a man crashed through a ground-floor window, staggered to his feet, and shot another man coming through the swinging doors. A third man stepped through the shattered window and shot the first man. He fell in the street. Even from their distance they could see his body twitching.

Fargo caught Annie glancing at him. Both females

moved their mounts closer to the Ovaro. He said to Tessa, "Do you still think this is your kind of place?"

She was slow in answering. "They won't hurt us, Annie. Don't be afraid."

"Don't bet on it," Fargo commented. "These men are rough and tough, not to mention mean. There are less than a dozen women in Creede and more than fifty men. The women are as tough as the men. Anything goes in Creede. We will stop long enough to buy you girls guns."

"Guns," Tessa gasped.

"Yep. To protect your asses with."

"Mr. Fargo, watch your language," Annie admonished.

Fargo looked at her and said wryly, "Unless you want to sleep with me and my Colt. Do you?"

Annie shook her head, but Tessa allowed it was a good idea. Fargo told them he didn't intend to sleep with them. He insisted on buying the guns.

A knot of men came out of the saloon to watch the new arrivals ride into town. A younger, rawboned man swung off the porch and grabbed Annie by the thigh and slurred drunkenly, "Rosie is gonna have you, li'l darling. I've got just what you need to make you happy."

Kicking at him, Annie screamed, "Get your hands off me, you filthy little man."

Fargo dropped back, moved around her horse, and drew his Colt, growling, "She said for you to take your hands away. I suggest you do just that, unless you prefer that I shoot them off your wrists."

Two of the men on the porch drew their revolvers and stepped into the street. One snarled, "Rosie was just feeling the little whore. Besides, you got two, and we aim to relieve you of both of 'em."

Fargo swung the Colt around and fired one shot into the dirt between the man's boots and growled, "Don't threaten me, mister. Next time I'll kill you. Now, I suggest you holster those guns and go back in the saloon before I get real mad. You too, Rosie."

Rosie held up his hands. Smiling hugely, he said, "Aw, hell, big man, we didn't intend to get you all riled up."

Rosie turned to walk away, then spun around suddenly. His six-gun was coming out of its holster when

Fargo slapped him in the head with the Colt. The others watched Fargo swing the Colt onto them. Fargo advised, "Little boys shouldn't play with men unless they're prepared to pay the penalties. Get out of here, and take Rosie with you." He dropped his Colt in its holster and told the cousins to go on.

They rode around the body lying in the street and angled toward the small sod-roofed general store. Fargo led the girls inside and asked the fuzzy-faced old man behind the counter if he had any Smith & Wessons. He placed several on the counter. Fargo inspected them, then chose two. "I'll need a box of bullets for each," he said, "and holsters and the shortest gun belts you have."

Fuzzy-face reached behind and removed two boxes of shells from one shelf, the gun belts from the one below it. Fargo handed the gun belts to the females, saying, "Here, see if they fit,"

With adjustments, both were okay, although they rode low on the girls' hips. Fargo inserted cartridges in the chambers, then put the rest in the leather holders on the gun belts. He paid the man.

Walking out of the store, Fargo asked, "Either of you ladies ever fire a handgun?"

Tessa allowed she had, once. Before mounting up, he had them fire one round down the street. "Sleep with them under your pillow," he suggested. "And sleep lightly from here on."

They rode to a single-story hotel across from the saloon. Upon entering, they passed two giggling women and four tipsy men. All wore gun belts. Each woman was clutching two of the men. One of the men took his hat off and tried a bow that didn't work out. He said, " 'Evening, girls. I' ll come back later and bend you over."

The woman he was with grabbed Tessa's arm and snarled, "Like shit, he will. Over my dead body. You fuck with Ben and your scrawny asses are all mine. Hear me, honey?"

Tessa wrenched her arm free and backed into Fargo's arms. They watched the sextet stagger out the door. Fargo quipped, "Wasn't that exciting?"

"No," Tessa mumbled.

Fargo paid for two room keys and asked for them to be adjoining.

The bearded clerk glanced at the two women, then at him, and asked, "Short time or all night?"

"We're here to sleep, not—"

"And we don't want to be disturbed," Annie cut in emphatically.

The clerk showed her a screwed-up face as he replied, "Lady, this is a hotel, not a liberry. I don't promise nothing." His eyes drifted onto Fargo. "You still want the rooms?"

Tessa answered by reaching over and taking the keys from the man.

"Rooms, six and eight," he grunted. "Down the hall, on your left."

While Fargo was installing them in room eight, somebody nudged him in the ribs. He twisted around, his gun hand instinctively going to the Colt.

A naked woman stood in the doorway. She shot him a smile and said, "Got a match, big boy?" She held up a badly rolled cigarette. She looked into his eyes while he struck a match on his thumbnail and lit her cigarette. Taking a puff, she said, "Thanks." Then she looked past him to Tessa and Annie. "I see you have mighty pretty company," she said to Fargo. "Me, too. I got me two rich ones. No matches, though."

They watched her enter the door across the dimly lit hallway. Fargo shut their door and stepped to the window. Parting the flimsy, dirty curtains, he checked the window's lock. Tightening it, he told them, "Lock your door when I leave. Don't let anybody in but me. I'll be over at the saloon for about an hour. I'll knock on my wall when I come back."

"I'm scared," Tessa said. "I want out of this town. First I watched a man get shot down in the street, then that man felt Annie. Annie, weren't you scared?"

"Worse has happened to me." Annie shot a hard look at Fargo.

He could sympathize with her. But what had been done, had been done. At least he killed the bastards. Nonetheless, Annie's hurt would be long-lasting.

Tessa went on, "Those two nasty women tried to pick a fight with me. Will it never end?"

"At daylight," he said. "The night can be evil around here. Annie, do you want me to stay here during the night?"

"No," she said. "I now have a gun, thank you."

As he looked into the hallway, Annie lit the lamp. Tessa shut the door. He waited until he heard it be locked, then left through the door at the end of the hall. He scanned the darkness behind the hotel, saw nothing amiss, then walked alongside the side having the windows. He paused to see if he could look through the thin curtain. Tessa's vague form was removing her shirt. He tapped on the windowpane and said, "Blow out the lamp."

She jumped, startled. Annie blew it out.

Fargo headed for the noisy saloon.

12

A long line of horses stood outside the saloon. Fargo walked behind them to see if he could recognize any. Near the end, he found that he did: Sheriff Warren's and Deputy Justin's. Armed with that knowledge, he stepped to the double doors and paused to scan the room.

The saloon was packed with rowdy people. The cigar and cigarette smoke was so dense that it was impossible to recognize anyone any farther than midway in the room. Two burly bartenders stayed busy filling beer mugs and whiskey glasses, shoving them along the bartop as quickly as the order was filled. Two others worked among the tables. Fargo saw four saloon girls and suspected there would be more in the back rooms. There was no second level. A long mirror, long since shattered by bullets, hung behind the bar. Spittoons overflowed onto the grimy, blackened wood floor. The place stunk to the high heavens. Fargo stepped inside.

He wedged in between two derelicts at the end of the bar so he could view the faces crowded down its full length. A bartender looked at him, nodded, signaling for his order. Fargo raised his palm to the height of a beer mug. The bartender slid a full mug of beer to him and held up ten fingers. Fargo slid a dime to him. Drinking his beer, he studied faces through the blue haze, first those lining the bar. He made out Rosie's about halfway down its length. Then the pair he'd backed down standing near the far end.

He moved to a table to ostensibly watch a game of five-card draw while looking for other faces he would recognize. He believed he saw the sheriff and deputy seated at a table in the back corner. They had their backs to the corner. A saloon girl was seated at the table with her back to Fargo. Three other men were also there. Fargo moved to another table to get a closer look.

They were so preoccupied with their own conversation that they didn't notice him. The Trailsman put his wild-creature hearing to work, eased a table closer, and through the din heard the sheriff say, "We'll get the assholes if we have to chase them into the mountains."

The woman said, "You're the biggest bunch of clumsy fools I've ever hired."

Now Fargo recognized the three bank robbers who got away. One of them, Blevins, shifted uncomfortably in his chair and said, "Aw, Warren, they was on us before we knew it. We'll get 'em yet. Wait and see."

Fargo had heard enough. He decided there were too many innocent people in the room for him to have it out with the sheriff and the others. He took a step backward, turned, and started walking toward the double doors, figuring on confronting them out in the street.

Sheriff Warren snarled, "Hold it right there, mister. Turn around so I can see your face. Don't touch your gun."

The customers in the immediate area instantly ceased all conversation. A heartbeat later they scattered for safety. When so many chairs were shoved back or overturned during their hasty retreat, the others in the saloon knew something bad was happening. A few hurried outside. The rest turned and looked, then quickly moved out of the line of fire. Fargo found himself standing alone.

He turned slowly and faced five drawn guns.

Widow Loch took one fast look at him, then knocked over the chair when she fled toward the bar. As she ran, she blocked three of the guns. In that instant, Fargo seized the moment, dived left, and began rolling on the floor.

Slugs chewed into chairs, tables, and woodwork.

He whipped out his Colt and fired twice blindly to intimidate them. He heard one round thud into the back wall, the other bury into flesh.

The gunmen scattered and continued to shoot at him.

Fargo toppled a poker table and immediately rolled away from it. Bullets dug into the tabletop. He saw he'd wounded Blevins in the left shoulder. This time Fargo shot him in the heart. The deputy swung his gun onto him. Fargo was faster. One bullet was all it took to expose the deputy's brains. The others broke off and ran down the hallway and out the back door.

Coming to his feet, he heard Rosie say, "You ain't so tough."

Fargo spun and saw three guns aimed at him.

"Drop that big Colt of yours, mister," Rosie commanded as he came toward Fargo.

Fargo dropped the Colt. The two backing up Rosie stood side by side. A big mistake, Fargo thought.

Rosie approached close enough that Fargo could smell the alcohol on the man's breath. Rosie said, "You hit me for doing nothing, mister. Now, I'll let you feel it the same way before I blow your head off."

Fargo rolled in advance of Rosie's onrushing revolver. The glancing blow still hurt, yes, and Fargo sank to his knees. He clutched Rosie's gun belt with one hand and drew the Arkansas toothpick with the other.

Rosie's eyes bulged and he screamed quite soberly as the stiletto sliced open his stomach. Blood and intestines gushed out on Fargo. He jerked the gun out of Rosie's dying hand and shot both would-be gunslingers in the chest. "Show's over, folks," Fargo said calmly.

He moved to the uncrowded bar and asked a bartender for a wet rag to clean the blood off his clothes.

Handing it to him, the bartender said, "Those punks gunned down Zack Ellman earlier. Zack was a nice, gentle man. Rare traits for around here." He poured a mugful of beer and refused payment for it.

"Did you see where the woman sitting with the first group went?"

"Are you gonna kill her, too?" The bartender frowned.

"I don't kill women unless they're pointing a gun at me," Fargo replied.

"She went in Lola's room. Second door on the left."

Fargo nodded, downed his beer, then went to the door. He found it locked and said, "Mrs. Loch, you and

I need to have a little talk. Let me in or I'll kick the door down. I won't hurt you."

The door opened slowly. Shaking like an aspen leaf, Marlena Loch looked at him through frightened brown eyes. He nodded and closed the door. She immediately retreated into a corner. He positioned the only straight-back chair to face her and sat. "Where is the bank's money," he asked quietly. "And you better not lie to me."

The woman dropped to her knees. Tears ran down her cheeks as she wrung her hands. Finally, she said in a trembly voice, "I don't know. Warren has it."

"Come, now, you can do better than that. I said, don't lie to me." He crossed his legs.

The movement startled her into confessing, "Two men, drifters—"

"Were they wearing dusters?" he interrupted. "Both of them young?"

"Yes. They appeared when we were dividing the money. I told Warren he should have one of the others stand guard while we were dividing it. But he didn't listen to me."

"So they go the drop on you all and took the money?"

"Yes. They were on us before we realized it. They put the money in the bags after disarming us and throwing the weapons into thickets."

"Which way did they go?"

"To the rainbow? Or something that sounded like that. I didn't understand. They said their brothers at the rainbow would be pleased. When they left, they headed toward Creede. That's why we were there."

"Madam, I suggest you travel with better company. Go home and make a new life for yourself. Stop being so greedy."

"But, but, I'm flat broke. I don't have money enough to get back home."

Rising, Fargo said, "Then you're in a hell of a fix stuck in this town. I suggest you start walking back to the Gap." At the door he added what Angus McCord would say, "Where's there's a little peace and tranquillity." He left her kneeling and sobbing and went to the bar.

"I need new clothes," he told the bartender. "Is the owner of the general store in here?"

The bartender said, "Sam's playing poker at that table over by the wall."

Fargo went to Sam and waited until the next shuffle-up before saying, "Sam, you want to recover some of your losses? I'm Skye Fargo and I need to buy some clothes."

Sam looked at the bloodstained shirt and grinned. Pushing back from the table, he told the card players, "Watch my money. Hold my seat for me. I'll be right back."

Fargo put a hand on Sam's shoulder to keep him from rising, and said, "Count to ten before standing, then walk to your store. I'll meet you there."

Sam counted as he watched Fargo go to the bar, then drift toward the back door.

Fargo knew Warren and the two bank robbers would be hiding in the dark, waiting for him to come out the front door of the saloon. As he stepped outside, he drew his Colt, swung around the framework, and flattened his back against the wall. He saw nobody, heard no movement. Moving swiftly, silently, he went behind the saloon and peered around the corner. He saw nobody standing at the far end of the saloon. He moved behind the next building, repeated his caution, and saw nobody. Encouraged, he ran stealthily around the third structure, crossed the darkened street, and found the back door to the general store. He tapped on it until Sam came to investigate. Fargo whispered, "It's me, Fargo. Open the door."

The door swung out. Fargo slipped inside. Within minutes he was pulling on new underwear, Levi's, and a shirt. As he was paying Sam, one of the bank robbers broke out a front windowpane and shot at him. The bullet grazed hair sticking out from under his hat. Fargo had his Colt drawn instantly and shot at the shadowy form. He heard somebody kicking in the back door. Sam got to safety behind bags of feed.

Caught in the middle, Fargo started backing into a corner. That's when he heard Annie's high, piercing scream from inside the hotel.

Casting aside all caution, Fargo ran to the front door.

He yanked it open and came out with his gun blazing hot lead to intimidate them.

He crouched as he ran along the front porch. A fusillade of bullets tore into the wall behind him. More splintered the entrance to the hotel as he dived into it, rolled to safety, and quickly reloaded. Bullets chewed into the lobby walls and counter as he ran down the darkened hallway to the cousins' door.

He plastered his back to the wall next to the door and reached for the knob. Turning it, he found the door already cracked. He shoved it wide open and swung inside the dark room. In the scant light that filtered through the skimpy curtains from the saloon across the street, he saw the Smith & Wessons lying on the bedsheet. Tessa and Annie were gone. They had put up a struggle: the one chair was overturned, so was the nightstand.

Fargo heard Annie scream again. This time it came from outside, from the back of the hotel. He ran to the back door and looked out. Horses were pounding away in the night, heading for the wilderness northwest of the tawdry little frontier town.

He turned to run to the Ovaro, hitched in front of the hotel. A slug sizzled past his head.

Warren shouted, "We have him trapped. Move in on him, Chance." Warren had shot at him from one side of the hallway opening. One of the bank robbers from the other. Both rounds missed by inches.

Fargo ducked and ran out the rear door. Chance opened fire, the bullets thudding into the wall behind Fargo. "He's out," Chance called to them. "Going down this side of the hotel."

Fargo clung to the side of the hotel, knowing Chance couldn't see him and dared not expose himself by following. He paused at the cousins' window, backed off, then dived through it. Scrambling to his feet, Fargo ducked into the lobby and leapt through the doorway.

Warren and a bank robber were standing in the middle of the street, watching the side of the building. They swung and fired when Fargo jumped onto the porch. He came off it firing rapidly at them, and unhitched the Ovaro. Swinging up into the saddle, he glimpsed Warren beating a hasty retreat back inside the saloon, the bank robber down on his knees, clutching his right upper arm. Chance ran out into the street and opened fire as the Ovaro raced into the darkness at the far end of the street. Fargo heard him call the wounded man Rupert.

Fargo reloaded as he rode into the night to intercept the riders who had taken Tessa and Annie. He reckoned they had no more than a five-minute lead on him. Riding double, they wouldn't go far before he caught up. He knew they would avoid rough terrain at night, especially woods, for fear of running into a tree, so he stuck to open ground and raced on.

He fired twice into the air to let the girls know somebody was coming, reloaded, and strained to listen for one of them to scream. Annie's voice yelled from far ahead, "Help! Help us!"

"I'm coming," he shouted back, and nudged the Ovaro into a dead run.

The Ovaro ran right between Annie and Tessa before Fargo saw them sitting on the ground and could rein to a halt. He heard two horses running away in the night. He dismounted and went to the young women and asked, "You two all right?"

"Where were you?" Annie barked. "Don't look at or touch me," she spat venomously.

Standing there in the total darkness, he wondered why she would say that. Tessa explained, "She's buck-naked, Skye, darling. Me, too. They caught us with our drawers off."

"Who?" he asked, even though he was sure of the answer.

"Frank and Ray," Tessa said.

"Oh, how do you know?" he quizzed her.

"Er, uh, one called the other Ray, and Ray called him Frank. I was never so frightened in my whole life."

"Well, they're gone for now," he said. "Which of you wants to ride up front?"

"I do," Tessa answered eagerly.

"Hop on," he said. "Now, Annie, I'm going to have to lift you by your waist to put you on behind the saddle, unless, of course—"

"I'll climb up all by myself," she hastened to interrupt. "Please avert your eyes while I do, Mr. Fargo."

He turned his head and listened to her grunt her way up. He wondered what she would do to keep anyone from seeing her nakedness while going to her hotel room.

"The bedroll is uncomfortable," she complained.

Easing into the saddle, he muttered, "It's a long way back to the hotel, ma'am, but if you prefer walking, that's fine with me. Do you?"

"No," Annie mumbled bitterly.

"Aw, Annie, quit fussing," Tessa told her. She turned to face Fargo and said, "Annie's just afraid of you, Skye. For the life of me, I don't know why. Want me to sit closer to you, darling?"

She already had her butt, tattoo, and all fused tightly to his crotch. He wondered what more she could possibly want.

Tessa whispered, "If you will undo your fly, I'll raise up a mite."

"I heard that," Annie spat. "Tessa, you ought to be ashamed of yourself, talking like that. My word."

"No shame, dear cousin. Thrills. Only thrills to go with such a romantic night. I've never done it while in the saddle."

Fargo was glad Annie stayed silent after that brief exchange. Approaching the hotel, he avoided the light from the saloon as long as he could.

As they moved into the glow, Tessa asked Annie, "What will you do now, dear cousin?"

Annie had an answer ready. "Mr. Fargo, I need your shirt. Please hand it to me before proceeding any farther."

Chuckling, Fargo reined the Ovaro to a halt, pulled off his shirt, and gave it to her. "Tell me when you have it on," he said, "so I'll know when to proceed." After a pause, she told him to go on.

He crossed the street and rode behind the saloon. Dismounting, he told them to stay put while he went inside.

Annie said icily, "While you drink and carouse with the saloon girls?"

Fargo ignored the caustic remark. He went in and stood at the far end of the narrow hallway. He saw Warren, Chance, and Rupert at a table near a front window. They were watching the hotel. Rupert's right sleeve had been ripped off. His neckerchief covered the flesh wound.

Fargo caught a tall, redheaded whore's attention and motioned her to him.

Her hand went to his crotch and squeezed as she cooed, "My, my, what big balls you have. And so full. Want me to empty 'em, big man?"

He pulled her into the hallway and said, "No, but I need your room for the night."

Nonchalantly, as though it was done all the time, she replied, "It will cost you ten dollars, mister. Because, I'll have to use a room over in the hotel."

Handing her his room key and the ten, he said, "The room's paid up for the night."

The redhead's puzzled expression told him she was thinking, then why do you want my room? Finally, she blinked and said, "Third door on the right."

He watched her go back and be absorbed in the blue haze, then he went to the cousins. "Okay, ladies, we stay here for the night."

"Here?" Annie began to protest. "I'm not staying in another filthy saloon."

Fargo pulled her off the bedroll and growled, "Oh, yes, you are. And this time I'm staying in the whore's room with you whether or not you like it."

Annie backed away and watched openmouthed while he removed his bedroll. He led the Ovaro to a shed nearby and hitched him to the door handle. She watched him remove bedroll and saddlebags, then withdraw his Sharps from its saddle case and stride back to her. Fargo was past taking any more off her. He shoved her toward the door. Opening it, he told them, "Go to the second door on your left. Stay close to the wall. You first, Annie." When she cut hard eyes at him, he threatened, "I said for you to git."

Both girls flinched and reached for the door handle at

the same time. Fargo knocked Tessa's away and pulled her a pace backward. Annie parted the door slowly and peered inside. Fargo pushed her into the shadowy hallway, then nudged Tessa inside. They proceeded to the door without further rebellion from Annie. She stepped inside just as a man staggered out of the room across the hall. Stuffing his shirt in, he ogled Tessa, but shot Fargo a wink and slurred drunkenly, "Pardner, looks to me like you picked the best-looking bitch of the whole litter." The fellow patted Tessa's butt and then headed into the saloon.

Tessa said, "He was a nice man."

Fargo nudged her inside the room. He dropped the bedroll and saddlebags, groped his way to the side of the bed, and lit the lamp on the table next to it. Tessa closed the door and locked it. Annie backed into a corner.

Tessa sprawled invitingly on the bed and watched him spread his bedding in front of the door, then sit on it and bring a pint of whiskey out of his saddlebags. After taking a swig of it, he looked at Annie and said, "Earlier you asked where I was. Now I'm going to tell you. I was busy killing scum like those who captured and took you to their hideout in Diablo Canyon. I shot to death the man who grabbed your thigh. I shot to death the two men who threw down on me. And I shot to death one of the bank robbers and the sheriff's deputy. A lot of killing for one night. I'm lucky to still be alive."

"Oh, Skye, darling, we didn't know," Tessa apologized. "Come to bed and let me love on you, rub my soft breasts on your body."

Oddly, he thought, Annie didn't censure Tessa for offering her body to him. "I apologize for my cousin's unladylike conduct, Mr. Fargo," Annie began in a calm tone of voice. "But I want you to understand I'm a proper lady and expect to be treated as one. I have no intention, or desire, of, allowing you to wallow on me. You have my permission to remain on guard in the room while we sleep."

"Thank you, ma'am. And I want you to know the night's violence probably isn't over yet. I brought you in the back way because three bank robbers are in the saloon, keeping an eye on the hotel and your two horses out front. Sooner or later they will put two and two together, figure this is the only place where we could be, and start trying the doorknobs."

He drank half the whiskey, then pitched the bottle to Tessa.

Sleep came quickly to Fargo. His wild-creature hearing sent continuous sound messages to his brain. Therefore he heard, but didn't listen to, the diminishing noise levels out in the saloon. The pitch was such that it amounted to a babbling hum. Slowly, ever so slowly, the monotonous drone softened until it vanished altogether. In that silence Fargo's hearing became even more sensitive, his brain even more alert.

The doorknob above his head barely twisted. The catch made a breath sound that would have been inaudible to most ears. Tessa's soft, rhythmical breathings easily absorbed the sound. But Fargo's ears heard it and sent a warning signal to his brain. His eyes snapped open instantly.

He looked at the knob. His right hand went to and gripped his Colt without making a whisper of a sound. As he watched the knob, somebody turned it a tad more, enough so that he heard the catch slip free. When that slight sound came, he used it to mask the metallic click of his thumbing back the hammer. Aiming the gun at dead center on the door, he rose quietly, pulled the bedroll away just as gently, and stepped to one side. The person pushed gently on the door—then harder when the inside latch held.

In one swift movement Fargo slipped the latch and jerked the door open. Caught off-balance by the suddenness of his action, the tall redhead lost her grip on the knob. She gasped and braced herself on the door's framework. Fargo looked at her badly bruised face and disheveled condition and lowered the Colt.

Warren stepped from the heavy shadows consuming the hallway. So did Chance and Rupert. All pointed six-guns at Fargo's chest.

The redhead looked at Fargo through puffed, bloodshot eyes that were all but closed from the beating she had taken. The apologetic expression on her battered face conveyed more to him than words could possibly say.

Warren's free hand shot to her hair. He snatched her out of the way and flung her to the floor behind him. Glancing to the cousins sound asleep on the bed, he growled to Fargo, "Shithead, it's high time you died."

As Warren spoke, two things happened simultaneously: Annie emitted an ear-shattering scream, and the door directly across the hall burst open.

Startled, Warren blinked, heeled the butt of his revolver, and jerked the trigger. The hot, speeding slug missed Fargo's shoulder by a centimeter, then knocked a hunk of wood out of the wall beyond the bed.

Fargo glimpsed Widow Loch standing in the doorway across the hall. She was raising a pistol. He slammed the door shut in Warren's face and dropped the latch. Fargo fired two rounds into the door, then plastered his back to the wall next to it.

He didn't have to warn the young women to get out of the line of fire; they were already on the floor on the far side of the bed.

Six answering bullets splintered through the door. No sooner had the sounds of the gunfire rumbled into the saloon than Fargo heard the pistol bark twice. A man yelled painfully. The pistol shots were instantly followed by a single, louder retort.

A flurry of bootsteps scurrying away reverberated in the hall. Fargo unlatched and swung the door open. He dived out into the hallway. Rupert was fast escaping out the rear entrance. Fargo brought his Colt up and fired twice at the fleeing man, but missed. Three shots were returned through the doorway. All buzzed above Fargo and ricocheted off walls. Then there was silence.

The pungent odor of gunpowder filled the narrow hallway. Reloading, Fargo rose and looked through the gunsmoke. The redhead was slumped against a wall sobbing softly. Marlena Loch lay in her doorway. She clutched the bloodstained front of her bloomers where one of them had put a bullet in her stomach. Blood seeped between her fingers. Widow Loch wouldn't be going home.

Fargo squatted beside her. She murmured, "I tried to shoot Warren, but one of the others got in the way. Sorry."

"You did fine," Fargo told her, but Marlena had taken her final breath. He dragged a thumb and forefinger over her eyelids, then stood.

Whores and their customers peered out of their doorways. He told them it was all over and asked the men to dispose of the widow's body. A trail of blood led out the back door, red testimony that she had, indeed, wounded one of them.

Annie and Tessa stood in the doorway. He told them it was time to leave, and asked Tessa to roll up his bedding and bring it and his saddlebags along; then he reached inside the room and got the Sharps, which was leaning against the wall. At the back door he scanned the darkness and listened for movement before stepping outside. The Ovaro knickered lowly.

The girls joined him as he unhitched the stallion. Putting the saddlebags and bedroll in place, he said, "The danger isn't over, ladies. We still have to fetch your clothes, then get out of Creede. I know three of them are alive, albeit one is bleeding. I have yet to determine why they want me so badly as to risk their lives." He didn't volunteer he suspected that it had to do with something Frank or Ray told them when they "stole" the stolen money. He wished he'd thought to ask the widow. He'd had two opportunities. Now there would be no more.

Annie said, "Mr. Fargo, I'm chilled. Can we please go?"

He glanced at her and started walking a circuitous route that would keep them veiled in the dark and bring them to the rear of the hotel. On the way the only sounds they heard were two dogs barking and roosters exchanging crowings. Those of the dogs came from far down the street as they crossed it. If the outlaws were there, Fargo reckoned he and the girls would have plenty of time. Arriving at the rear of the hotel, he told them to wait while he checked the hall.

Fargo saw nobody in the hallway, neither did he hear a sound. He motioned the young women forward. He stood guard in the hallway while they went in and dressed.

Annie handed him his shirt and said quite loudly, "Thank you, Mr. Fargo."

The door across the hall parted. The woman who had asked for a match stepped out. She said, "My two, er, friends earlier? I didn't know they were thieves till later. They got to bragging about stealing those bags of money from some men on their way to town. They even showed it to me."

"How did they know these women had the room across the hall?" Fargo asked.

She glanced at the cousins and said, "I told them you had two good-looking young ladies in the room across the hall. I was bragging on you. I watched them try the door. When they found it locked, one of them went to the lobby and got the extra key. Then all hell broke loose."

"What all did they say while bragging?" Fargo pressed.

"Oh, mostly how they had surprised these people with the money. They said they threw them off the track. The younger one—I think his name was Ray—laughed and told the other that was clever thinking on his part. They really bragged. Ended up giving me a whole hunnert dollars."

"The part about clever thinking? What did they say, specifically?" Fargo was sure he knew her answer, but wanted to be positive.

She looked at Fargo. A smile played on her face as she said, "That you and two young whores sent them. Ray said you were the ringleader. He said that if they, meaning the people with the bags of money, came after them, you would kill them. Got another match?" She held up another cigarette.

Fargo gave her three, then nodded for the cousins to head for the back door. He said, "Wait inside till you hear me coming with your horses."

He went to the lobby and looked outside. Seeing nobody, he slipped between the horses and unhitched them. He was leading the horses alongside the hotel when two shots rang out, but the bullets whizzed harmlessly overhead. Drawing his Colt, Fargo hurried the horses to the back door and told the girls to mount up and head for the trail northwest of town.

A bullet slammed into a shed back of the hotel as he swung up into his saddle. He emptied the Colt down along the side of the hotel, then set the Ovaro to running.

Dawn was breaking when he caught up with the fast-riding cousins.

13

A gorgeous sun peaked over the mountains. Fargo slowed his pace, then reined the Ovaro to a halt. Turning in the saddle, he watched the sunrise. He smiled at Annie and Tessa and commented, "This is why I enjoy the wilderness so much. The mornings are the best times. Part of nature awakens while the other part goes to sleep. Man has to be careful about disturbing the perfect balance, the order that nature takes care of all by itself. Harmony exists on this side of Creede, unless, of course, man violates it."

Annie cocked her head and squinted at him. "Mr. Fargo, I didn't know you had the mind of a poet."

Tessa added, "And a body of steel. Annie, why don't you show him your butt and tell what goes with the tattoo? Skye, darling, I won't mind if you pull her off that horse and strip—"

"Tessa, you shut up," Annie cried. "Don't put ideas in his head." She stared coldly at Fargo, as though he might try.

Tessa laughed. "Oh, me, dear Annie. What am I going to do with you? You will age to become a dried-up, prune-faced old biddy. Darling, you have to live a little. Enjoy, while you're still young."

"Like you do?" Annie scoffed.

"Yes."

"No, thanks." Annie flashed her eyes Fargo's way. "I don't want any man laying his hands on me."

"Well, darling, all I have to say is, you're missing a lot of thrills. Letting him look at your ass doesn't mean—"

"Tessa, I said for you to shut up. I don't appreciate that kind of talk."

Shaking her head slowly, Tessa grimaced. After five minutes' silence she asked, "Skye, darling, where are you taking us?"

"To the gates of hell." He grinned and threw her a wink. Of course he planned on going up Henson's Creek, but he didn't tell her that. He figured the stream was three days away. The deeper he got Annie into the wilderness, the more she would rely on him, he reasoned. Maybe then she would at least reveal the instructions applicable to the tattooed map. He'd find a way to make her tell. He'd better, he told himself, otherwise they'd wander, searching until cold weather set in.

They were riding through a broad valley filled with colorful wildflowers. Fargo's gaze swept up the mountains on either side of the long, meandering valley. A soft grin formed on his lips as he thought of Angus McCord. Angus would appreciate being here. The angle of the sun, coupled with the irregular shape of the mountains on Fargo's left, painted the mountain forest of pine different shades and hues of green. A golden streak of aspen rushed up the mountainside, ending as abruptly as it began. A few cottonball clouds floated over the summits in the west. Otherwise, the azure sky went uninterrupted.

Four tree swallows, moving across the valley, flew graceful patterns low over the valley floor. They drew Fargo's attention to the wildflowers. Pink plumes encompassed an acre or more of fireweed. Calliope hummingbirds hovered among the Indian paintbrush that grew in profusion here. A seemingly endless number of bees worked among the low-growing yellow evening primrose on his right. A western jumping mouse, almost unseen by Fargo, was cutting the tender stem of a beardtongue with its teeth, preliminary to getting at the seeds. The blaze of color, not unlike an artist's palette, melded the closer it got to the base of the mountain.

The scents of the wildflowers blended and created an ever-changing aroma. Fargo inhaled deeply of the delicate perfume rising off the valley floor. Lazy zephyrs brushed his hair, kissed his nose and lips.

Fargo looked behind to see if the riders were shadowing him, and how many. They were there, of course, watching and waiting, but he didn't see any of them. He continued to check behind from time to time until they left the valley and entered a mountain forest of lodgepole pine. They were on the first of a series of switchbacks leading up the mountain when muted sounds of pistol and rifle fire punctured the air. The sounds triggered a chuckle from Fargo. The two groups of outlaws had finally discovered each other.

Annie and Tessa snapped their pretty heads around to face the sounds, but the density of the pine trees prevented seeing any farther than thirty feet.

Fargo's calm voice told them, "Come along, ladies. Watch where you're going. There's nothing to worry about. They're just terrorizing one another."

Tessa replied nervously, "That's what you say. Me, I'm scared."

"What for?" Annie muttered. "Mr. Fargo will shoot them."

"Goddammit, Annie, I'm frightened. On this twisting trail, we don't have any running room. How much farther, Skye?"

"You forgot to add the darling." He chuckled.

"Skye, darling?" she hissed.

"That's better," he said. "I don't know how much farther. I haven't been in this forest before," he lied. "But your fear is well-founded. They could catch and murder us easy enough," he teased.

"Er, uh, how about letting Annie and I ride up front?"

"Can't do that," he answered. "Remember, I'm the trailblazer. I know how, you don't."

He heard Tessa groan.

The gunfire petered out. Fargo reckoned they'd gotten out of range of one another. He wondered if any had gotten killed or wounded. In any event, they now had a double problem: staying out of each other's way, and tracking at the same time. Their forward progress would be slow.

Halfway up the mountain they came to a small clearing that presented a view of the valley below. Fargo halted and dismounted. Squatting, he looked down and said, "Ladies, get off those horses. Come see a beautiful sight."

"Skye, darling, I think we should go on while the getting is good."

"No," he told her over his shoulder. "We need to rest the horses. They will need to do the same, else their horses will drop dead. You can use the bushes uphill." He heard them dismount.

Annie came to the edge of the overlook. After a few seconds, she said, "I've never seen anything this beautiful. Never in my entire life."

"Yes, it is lovely. Under different circumstances I would make camp here and spend a couple of days just looking down on the valley. It will be even more spectacluar when we get to the top."

"You've been here before, haven't you, Mr. Fargo?" When he nodded without looking at her, she continued, "How severe of a problem do we have with them? You don't appear all that concerned."

"You're right. I'm not. I know these trails, these forests, where I'm going and what to expect. They do not. That's my advantage. At best, the problem with them represents a mere nuisance. I can lose them anytime I wish."

Annie looked at him and asked the obvious, "Then why don't you?"

Continuing to gaze upon the long, broad swath of nature's beauty, he told her, "I'm leading them to their deaths. I'm taking them to Rainbow's End."

"Oh? And how do you figure on finding it?"

Now he looked over his shoulder at her and made eye contact. As though there was no question about it coming to pass, he said dryly, "Because you will show and tell me the way."

She spun and headed uphill. Over her shoulder she spat, "That's so much wishful thinking on your part, Mr. Fargo."

He stood and returned his gaze to the scene below. Momentarily, Tessa appeared next to him. She didn't look down when she asked, "Did she tell you?"

"No. But she will eventually. When I get her in a bad fix, a hopeless situation."

"You would do that?" Tessa asked incredulously.

Glancing at her worried expression, he said, "Have no fear, darling Tessa. I didn't say either of you would get hurt. For all I know, Annie will volunteer the information. Hope so. You talk to her about it."

"I have," Tessa lamented. "I've cajoled her, begged, insisted, and even threatened bodily harm. None of it did any good. What 'bad fix'? Can I help?"

Fargo shook his head. "No."

She saw him squint at the western horizon. "Skye, darling, please let me help you."

"Talk to her. Looks like we're in for it."

"What?" She glanced down the trail.

"Rain. Clouds are building in the west. That usually means rain. Feel how still the air is."

Annie came back. Tessa told her it was going to rain. When Annie started debating her, Fargo walked out of their sight among the trees and relieved himself. Walking to the horses, he looked westward again. He told the girls to saddle up, he wanted to make it to the crest before sundown.

They had made it three-quarters up the mountainside when a cool breeze ruffled their hair. By the time Fargo attained the rocky summit, the breeze had strengthened into wind that twisted and thrashed the pine. Lightning flashed in the onrushing leading edge of black, roiling clouds. Thunder boomed and rumbled down the valley far below.

He dismounted next to a huge boulder. "We'll camp here for the night. You ladies build a fire among those boulders while I'm making a lean-to. He took his bedroll and saddlebags to a wide spot between the boulders.

Tessa said, "Won't they see our fire?"

"No matter," he half-shouted into the strong wind. He hobbled the horses, then started breaking off lower limbs to make the lean-to.

While making the fire, they watched him peel the branches and use the thin strips to bind them snugly together. After making the roof, he put it across the tops of two boulders and secured it with his throwing rope. Glancing at them, he said, "Don't want it carried away in the wind. Make a pot of coffee, please." He spread the three bedrolls under the roof.

Annie said, "I don't like it. That thing won't keep the rain out."

Pulling a pint of whiskey from the saddlebags, he mused wryly, "It's better than what you had in Diablo Canyon. Remember?"

She watched him open the bottle and take a swig from it. He handed the bottle to Tessa and continued, "You were buck-naked then. Remember? You were so glad to get out of there that you didn't mind who saw your body."

"What you say is true, Mr. Fargo. In that instance I didn't have any choice. Now I do."

"Aw, hell, cuz, have a slug of this whiskey," Tessa said, holding the bottle out for her to take.

Annie looked at it. Fargo noticed her hand move less than an inch toward the bottle, then pull back. She wanted the warming liquid and was resisting the urge to partake of it. Fargo reached out and took it from Tessa's hand. After swilling from it, he opened a tin of beans and shared it with the girls. He'd set the near-empty bottle on the ground by the fire. Annie choked on a mouthful of beans. Her hand shot to the bottle. They watched her guzzle it dry. Fargo got a fresh bottle and passed it to Tessa to open and give to Annie, who was still choking. He slapped her back as she took a long pull from the bottle.

"Sorry," Annie finally muttered apologetically.

After that she shared the whiskey with them. The coffee brewed. Annie took the tin cup offered by Fargo but raised the bottle to her lips instead. Fargo reckoned the hot storm raging inside her was more fierce than the one bombarding her exterior. She pitched the empty bottle over her shoulder and held out her hand for another one. He gave her the gin.

Tessa observed rather tipsily, "Is this the bad fix?"

"No. It's called surviving the elements."

He watched Annie widen and bat her eyes, jerk her

head in short shakes. The gin was relaxing her, numbing her, and her brain was swirling. He knew she was only moments away from passing out. Tessa did too. She said, "Well, Skye, darling, it's time for bed. I'll sleep with you first. Annie gets seconds."

As she spoke, Annie collapsed in Fargo's arms.

Tessa quickly changed her order of things. "On second thought, I'll take seconds and thirds and . . ." She too slipped into unconsciousness and slumped facedown.

Fargo downed the remaining gin, then brought another bottle of whiskey from the saddlebags. It was going to be a stormy night, and he too desired to sleep through it. He tucked the women in their bedrolls, then got into his own. Fargo drifted to sleep listening to the wind screaming over the boulders, murderously loud thunder booms that shook the roof, and watching lightning playing in the low clouds.

A driving rain and moist lips jarred him awake. Annie was out of her bedroll, lying between him and Tessa. The young woman was sound asleep with her face to his. Fargo opened the bedroll and pulled her in beside him. She snuggled against him. While her fully clothed body pressed to him felt good, he refused to take advantage of her and went back to sleep.

A hard slap on his cheek snapped his eyes open. Annie, he saw, had delivered the blow. She knelt in the fog enshrouding the mountain's top and snarled, "How dare you to take liberties with me. Mr. Fargo, you are a despicable man. How dare you!"

Feeling the cheek, he sat up and growled, "Mount up. Both of you."

Tessa stirred, looked at them, and mumbled, "How good was she, you lying bastard?"

Annie's hands went to her belt buckle and fly an instant before she quipped, "He never got the chance to find out. I awoke just in time."

"Mount up," he repeated. He silently vowed that the next time she came and touched him, what happened as the consequence would be justified. He shoved Annie off his bedding and rolled it up tightly.

Ten minutes later they were picking their way down

the side of the foggy mountain. They broke out of the fog while riding on a narrow ledge about halfway down the mountain. The warm sun felt good on Fargo's face. The ledge gave a panoramic view of a series of mountain ranges, several of which were snow-peaked. For all the beauty of the splendid view, instant death was promised if any of their mounts made a misstep on the ledge. The sheer drop-off plunged at least five hundred feet. Fargo dismounted and told the women to do the same. He led the Ovaro to the far end of the ledge.

At the end of it, the terrain took a dramatic change. No longer were they confined to the switchbacks like those on the other side of the mountain, or the treacherous rocky ledges hidden by the fog on this side. A gentle slope lay before them all the way to the base of the mountain. Blue spruce interrupted by groves of quaking aspen dominated this side. A stream carved from millennia of spring thaws and rainfalls traced the contours at the bottom of the mountain they were on and the one next to it. The angle of the bright sun was such that it left the stream shining as though it were a glimmering silver ribbon. Numerous beavers' ponds shone mirrorlike in ravines on the two mountainsides.

Looking up into the dense fog that covered most of the dangerous ledge, Tessa commented, "Thank God that's behind us."

Fargo mounted up and replied, "Come along, ladies. We don't want them getting within rifle range of us."

Riding past a beaver pond, he heard Tessa say to Annie, "Doesn't that pond look inviting?" Then in a louder voice, she said, "Skye, darling, Annie and I need a bath."

He told her, "Wait until we get to the stream. There's plenty of pools. I can use one, you two another."

She grumbled, "I don't see why we should wait."

"No need to disturb the beavers," he grunted. He kept going.

Coming to the stream, he rode along its bank until he came to a pool from where he got a clear view of the ledge. Dismounting, he said, "This is as good a place as any. I'll go upstream. Rinse your clothes while you're at it." He withdrew his Sharps from its saddle case and headed upstream.

About a hundred yards away he found a place where he could watch over them. After bathing and washing his clothes, he walked back on the far bank. He found a large boulder surrounded by brush directly across from them. The sun had burned off the fog covering the mountaintop. He watched four riders arrive at the beginning of the ledge and halt. Two wore dusters. He reckoned they had made a deal after killing one of the outlaws. Fargo estimated it would take an hour and a half for them to reach the stream.

His gaze moved onto the women, who were close enough for him to see their nipples clearly whenever one of them stood in shallow water near the bank. In a few minutes Annie came out and stood on the bank with her back to him. Her tattoo would have been invisible to anyone else but him. He brought it into focus. When she knelt at the calm water's edge, he looked at the image reflected on water. Acting on impulse, he imagined the tattoo when flopped. He grinned, for he now knew positively the general location of Rainbow's End. Fargo pulled on his wet undershorts and Levi's and put on his hat. Rifle, shirt, boots, and socks in hand, he waded the stream.

Tessa gasped, "Oh, Skye, darling, you caught me without any clothes on."

Annie darted behind the bushes, holding her clothes, and shrieked, "Don't come near me, Mr. Fargo! You said—"

"I know what I said," he cut in. "Only thing is they are coming down the mountain." He pointed to the riders.

Tessa gasped, "Oh, my God! There's four of them." She hurried out of the pool.

Pulling on his damp socks, Fargo told them to hurry and get dressed. He had decided to put at least two hours between them and the riders. He would give them a small problem to solve, one that would slow them down.

Annie and Fargo were already dressed and in their saddles. Tessa was holding things up, still trying to squirm into her wet Levi's. Fargo told her, "Hell, bring them with you. They're going to get sopping wet anyhow." He and Annie headed upstream.

After a few minutes, Tessa caught up with them. Fargo saw that she had managed to get into the Levi's. He put the Ovaro into a lope and went upstream to where it widened and shallowed. There he entered it and rode in its center for about two miles before coming out in a wide, rocky spot on the far side. He led the girls straight up the mountainside and didn't halt until he reached the summit.

He dismounted in an outcrop and looked down. The riders were searching the banks to find where they came out. They were less than a mile away from finding it. He guessed he'd succeeded in gaining about two hours or more on them. He looked skyward, to the west, and saw thunderheads building. The position of the sun indicated the hour to be about five o'clock. If they were lucky, the storm promised by the ominous thunderheads wouldn't strike before they got off the mountain. Fargo scanned the northern horizon and easily picked out the landmarks tattooed on Annie's rump. Lake San Cristóbal shimmered diamondlike under the rays of the sun. To its right and higher, the mountain tarn Crystal Lake glittered. Far in the distance towered snow-capped Red Cloud beyond and to the left of San Cristóbal. Uncompahgre loomed beyond and to the right of Crystal Lake. Between the two lakes Henson's Creek emptied into the Gunnison. That was where he would find the mine. He also surmised the other two Barrow brothers and Baldy were already there.

Tessa said, "Skye, darling, I need to visit the bushes, but there's none up here."

He had planned to rest for ten minutes. Tessa's pained expression, coupled with her knocked knees, put him back in the saddle. He said, "You two will find me down the other side. Take your time, but don't tarry too long." He rode away.

They found him sitting on the ground in a small, grassy meadow, chewing on a blade of grass, watching the Ovaro graze. "Get off those horses," he said. "Let them rest and graze a few minutes. Tessa, I want to talk to you."

"Sure, Skye, darling. What about?"

He waited until she and Annie sat. "I want another look at your tattoo."

Annie got up and stomped into the aspen nearby. Tessa smiled as she unfastened her belt. "How do you want me, Skye, darling? Standing, lying on my tummy, or on my hands and knees? Please say on my hands and knees. Annie isn't watching."

"On your belly."

Assuming the position, she spread her legs wide and raised her hips slightly. He drew her legs back together and pressed down on her buttocks. Straddling her at the waist so he could view the six molelike tattoos upside down, he imagined what the arrangement would look like when flopped over. Two of the tattoos were spaced in a line farther apart than the rest. Dead center and slightly left was a mole dot. Horizontal to it and across the imaginary line fixed in his mind were the markers, and above them two more created a boxlike pattern. Above the outside dot stood a single one, which he believed represented the mine. Then he imagined the reflected image of the arrangement. The single dot was now below the box. The only things missing, if he had figured right, were the distances to the markers and the markers themselves. He would figure that out when he got to Henson's Creek.

Tessa muttered impatiently, "Skye, darling, are you going to look at my rear end all day?" Rolling over between his knees, she cooed, "What say I give you a hot thrill? All you have to do is unbutton your pants."

He was tempted to accommodate the young lass. But he rose instead and asked, "What is the marker farthermost to the left?"

"It's . . . , I told you I didn't remember."

He knew she was lying. For what reason he did not know. He made her a test offer, one that she would be hard-put to refuse. "I'll bed you in the grass if you remember and tell me."

Grim-jawed, Tessa pulled the Levi's on. Fargo walked

to the pinto, now knowing she had indeed lied. She missed the chance to tell him another lie and claim the marker was anything. He shook his head when easing into the saddle. He shouted for Annie to come back, then rode off the meadow and down the mountainside. They joined him moments later.

Tessa sulked all the way to the bottom. A raindrop broke her silence and stubborn attitude. "Skye, darling, where are you going to stop? I'm exhausted."

"Later," he began. "When I come to the lake. I want to lose them," he lied.

"The rain will wash away our tracks." The last part was true, although he knew the riders would eventually find them. Fargo needed extra time.

Time for Tessa to tell him the truth. Or run.

14

Dawn broke over Lake San Cristóbal. The lake itself was hidden beneath a thin layer of fog, but not the east bank, where Fargo had erected a lean-to for the cousins. He chose a knoll, among aspen far down the shoreline, on which to spread his bedroll.

Rolling it up, he looked at the low-hanging, dull-gray clouds. They promised more rain. He scanned the shoreline across the narrow lake. The Gunnison below the lake flowed too swiftly for them to swim it. He feared the strong current would carry one of the young women and her horse to her death . . . maybe both girls. Fully rested, the horses could swim the calm waters of the lake. That's why he hadn't stopped until he reached it.

Tessa complained all the way—nagged at him, in fact. So much so that Annie, tired of listening to her cousin's constant grumblings, told her to shut up. They had argued most venomously briefly. Tessa bitterly accused Annie of causing the whole problem. She even went so far as to say she wished Annie dead. Annie was quick to retaliate. She branded Tessa a bitch, a whore. Tessa laughed and said, "Look who's talking! You're dying to clamp your legs around Mr. Fargo. You told me so. Bitch! Whore!"

Then the complexion of Tessa's accusations suddenly changed, but not the acidity of them. "Describe the landmarks to him. Tell him. We will wander till kingdom come if you don't."

"No," Annie had responded. "He will murder us if I do."

Fargo recalled he had chuckled. "I know where I'm

going. Annie, you don't have to describe the landmarks. I've already seen them, and I didn't murder you."

Annie answered, "Mr. Fargo, you're trying to trick me. You don't know where we are any more than I."

After a long pause he had said, "You will see one of the landmarks up close in the morning."

That pronouncement brought an end to their bickering. Fargo rode on into the night's torrential downpour.

He secured the bedroll on the Ovaro and led him to the lean-to. He saw the cousins had put aside their differences for warmth. Both were deep inside one bedroll. Fargo coughed to awaken them. It didn't do any good. He nudged a rump with a boot tip and said, "Wake up, ladies. It's time for an early-morning swim."

From deep within Tessa groaned, "Leave us alone. We're tired."

He shoved the lean-to away and pulled back the top cover of the bedroll. Two mops of hair poked out. He grabbed a strand of Tessa's black hair and tugged it gently.

She came out kicking and clawing. "Goddammit, Fargo, I'm tired and sleepy."

Her outburst popped open Annie's eyes. Terror-stricken, she screamed, "Don't kill us. Please don't. I'll tell."

"No need, ma'am." He nodded toward the lake.

She sat and stared at the fog rising off the water. Tessa looked down its length. She asked, "Where are we?"

"On the eastern shore of the biggest blue tattoo, Lake San Cristóbal."

He heard Annie suck in a breath and saw her smile. Tessa asked, "How far behind us do you suppose those men are?"

"Not far, if they rode all night." He knew the riders were damn close. His eyes had snapped open when a horse somewhere up on the slope had whinnied. "Find a bush, then make your horses ready for the trail. You'll find me down the bank a ways." He mounted up and rode off.

Fargo chose the narrowest place to cross—just above where the lake spilled into the river. He was studying it when the cousins rode up to him. "This is the place," he told them. "Dismount and lead your horses out into the water. It's shallow at first, but deepens fast. Hang on to your saddlehorns when you lose footing. The horses will do the rest. Don't panic and start swimming. You'll never make it to the bank." He led the stallion into the fog-covered water.

Glancing behind, he saw them still standing on the bank. He stopped and coaxed them to enter, saying he would wait for them. Annie came first. When she was abreast of him, Tessa said, "I'm afraid. I can't swim."

"Can you?" he asked Annie.

She shook her head.

"Does Tessa know you can't?"

She nodded.

"Are you afraid?"

Again, she nodded.

He walked the Ovaro till his foot found the drop-off, then he motioned Annie forward until she was alongside him. "Get a good grip on the saddlehorn," he said in a soothing tone of voice. When she did, he slapped the dun's rump. He watched the horse swim through the wispy fog and take Annie onto the bank.

Motioning Tessa forward, he challenged, "See how simple and easy it is? Trust your horse."

She shook her head.

He led the pinto to her and grunted in a no-nonsense tone, "Come on. You'll do it if I have to drag you."

"Oh, Skye, I'm afraid I'll drown."

He grabbed and shook her. She rebelled. He slapped her. While she was stunned, he led her and the chestnut to the dropoff, then whistled to the Ovaro. He came to Fargo immediately. Fargo put her hands on the pommel. She was clearly terrified as her grip tightened. Fargo said, "I'll be right behind you, honey," and slapped the chestnut's flanks.

The horse lurched. Tessa hung on with one hand and screamed, "It's over my head. I'm drowning."

Halfway across she let go and disappeared under the fog. Fargo swam to where she disappeared and dived to find her. She clutched him and started struggling. He surfaced with her, swam to the Ovaro, and threw her belly-down across the saddle. As the powerful stallion took them ashore, Tessa continued to scream. Fargo pulled her off the saddle and set her on the ground.

Annie said it true, "What with all her screaming, those men have surely seen us."

Tessa gasped for air and replied, "So what?"

Fargo scanned the slope across the lake. The riders would be on the bank shortly. He told the women to mount up, that the mine was near and he wanted to find it before the clouds dumped rain.

He followed the river to where Henson's Creek emptied into it. There he turned and rode up Henson's Creek. He knew the creek ended in a series of waterfalls about sixteen miles away, after meandering in the crevices. They were truly in high country now. He had reasoned the tattoo outside the farthest-spaced trio on Tessa's buttock cheek represented a key marker, the starting point that led to all others. The fartherest-spaced two had to be Henson's Creek. If the creek's full length was represented—and he believed that it was—then the placement of the outside tattoo followed that the marker would be found about midway up the stream.

In places the creek widened and ran shallow over pebbles and rocks. In others it narrowed and gushed between massive boulders. Forests of blue spruce, pine, and stately Douglas fir covered the steep mountainsides and ended at the water's edge. In the wider spots grew groves of aspen. Ravines and gulches carved from runoffs of rain were plentiful, widened by the numerous landslides and the jumble of fallen timber they caused.

After going upstream about six miles, Fargo dropped back and rode alongside Tessa. Surreptitiously, he watched her eyes.

A short time later, he saw her eyes flare. He followed the line of her gaze. A huge, elongated, smooth boulder protruded from a sheer wall of rock about a hundred feet above the floor of the narrower canyon, and more than a hundred yards in front of them.

Approaching the dark promontory, he saw it pointed to a very wide gulch that curved out of sight on the mountainside. The gulch widened considerably where it flattened and met the creek.

Passing under the mammoth stone, Tessa said, "Skye, darling, I need to find a bush. You and Annie don't have to wait for me. I'll catch up shortly."

He nodded and kept going. Rounding a bend, he reined to a halt and dismounted among aspen. He suggested Annie do the same. She slid from the saddle and went to the water's edge to wait. Fargo joined her. He skipped a few flat rocks over the surface of the stream, then studied the clouds roiling overhead.

"Will it rain?" she asked.

"A gully-washer," he answered.

They heard a whistle high on the mountainside across the stream. She glanced widened eyes at him. He saw they were filled with fear. "Nothing to be frightened about," he said. "It's only a bull elk telling his harem of our presence."

She sighed, relieved, and said, "I wish Tessa would hurry."

"Tessa isn't coming," he replied, and skipped another rock.

"Isn't coming," she gasped. "What do you mean by that, Mr. Fargo?"

"Tessa is halfway to Rainbow's End by this time."

"The mine? How do you know that?"

Squatting, he told her, "Those four riders were right behind us. They should have been here by now. Tessa waited for them. She's showing them the way to the mine."

"How dare you to say such a thing! Mr. Fargo, you're mistaken." Annie hurried to the dun.

Fargo caught up to her just as she put her left foot in the stirrup. When he grabbed her arm, she gasped, "No! Please don't rape and murder me." She started crying.

Fargo took her by the shoulders and shook her.

Annie whimpered, "Don't. Please don't do this to me." She broke free and ran stumbling into the creek.

He caught her on the far bank. She fought him, beat her little fists on his chest until she tired and slumped in his arms. He embraced her to hold her up and said, "I'm not going to hurt or violate you, Annie. What I said about Tessa is true."

Panting sobs, she asked weakly, "Mr. Fargo, Tessa is my only living relative. You're accusing her of—"

"No," he hurried to interrupt. "Tessa's father, your uncle, survived the massacre."

Annie mustered up a burst of strength. Breaking his embrace, she looked at him and said, "Uncle Charlie's alive? How do you know that? Why didn't he save me from Vásquez? Mr. Fargo, I don't believe you. You're just being mean to me." Annie spun and headed back to the aspen grove.

She stopped abruptly in midstream when he said, "You were supposed to die during the massacre."

Turning to face him, he saw her frown. After a thoughtful moment, she asked, "How do you know that? Who told you I was 'supposed to die?' "

The tone in her voice indicated to him that she was ready to listen with an open mind. He described Baldy to her. Annie's expression conveyed that Baldy was, indeed, her Uncle Charlie. "Shortly after the massacre, I saw him in the saloon at Beaver's Pond. He was at a table talking with the four Barrow brothers. Uncle Charlie and two of the Barrows are at the mine right now. They left Frank and Ray behind to kill you in the event I found and brought you back. Vásquez made a mistake when he didn't kill you at the wagons. Coming out of Diablo Canyon, he tried to correct his error. Remember? He shot at you. Not at any of the other women."

Annie sank to her knees. He watched her obviously think about what he'd just said. Slapping the water, she said bitterly, "Yes, yes, I see it now. But what about my cousin? Uncle Charlie didn't meet her in Wagon Wheel Gap."

"Frank and Ray did. She told them she didn't know the location of Rainbow's End. You had never described the landmarks. Correct?"

Annie stood and came to him. She was calm now. "No, never. What does it mean?"

"It means Charlie presumed you had told her. Otherwise, there's no logical answer for the Barrows not continuing to try to kill you. Or Tessa trying to pry the information out of you. She was desperate to know—so desperate that she got you drunk and showed me your tattoos."

Annie's brow furrowed as she said lamely, "In Miss Candy's Saloon."

Nodding, Fargo replied, "That's right. You and Tessa were slumped over a poker table, nude and passed out."

"Mr. Fargo, I owe you an apology for the manner in which I've treated you. I now know you are an honorable man, one who keeps his promises to a dying person. I intend to make my manners right by you." She embraced him and raised on tiptoes and kissed him on the mouth.

He cradled her in his powerful arms and carried her to their horses. She murmured and mewed little love sounds as she continued to kiss him, pouring out her passion. She had released him from his earlier vow by encouraging him with her lips and tongue, inviting him to take her.

With those hot moist lips caressing his, Fargo lowered her to the cool grass among the aspen. Holding their kiss, they shucked their clothes. He rolled between her legs and placed his throbbing manhood between her begging lower lips. Her breathing quickened in anticipation of the entry. She whispered, "What Tessa said about me desiring you was true. I hated and hungered for you at the same time."

"I know," he said, and thrust.

Her hips raised to help the penetration. She started squirming him fully into the hot, slickened and tight tunnel. Annie moaned her joy, "Yes, yes, oh, yes. That feels good, really good."

He felt her legs come up and rake his sides. She began bucking and swaying her hips slowly. He took her right breast into his mouth and sucked. She whimpered, "Oh, oh, don't stop. You're making me see beautiful stars. That's it, nurse on the nipple. Nurse on it . . . Aah . . . harder, Mr. Fargo. Suck it harder."

He felt her first orgasm seize his shaft. She shuddered as it happened, and moaned, "Oh, God, don't stop. Go deeper. Go faster and harder."

Moving to the left breast, he started thrusting harder, going deeper and faster. Her legs came up and her heels dug into his shoulders, positioning her channel for maximum penetration. When the base of his manhood parted her lower lips, she gasped, "Oh, my God . . . oh, my God . . . you're in me all the way . . . and it feels wonderful."

She had another orgasm, mightier than the first, and shrieked between clinched teeth throughout the pleasurable occurrence. When it passed, she lowered her feet and dug her heels into his hard buttocks. Gyrating wildly, she bucked until he gushed his hotness. It triggered a spasm down the length of her sheath, one that milked him dry.

Annie pressed her lips to his and kissed him openmouthed until he softened. Only then did she lower her legs to the grass and break the kiss, to look into his eyes and smile and say, "Tessa told me you were the best she ever had. I didn't believe her. Now I do. Thank you, Mr. Fargo, for giving me so much pleasure. It is a joy that I will remember forever."

He kissed both breasts, then rose, saying, "My pleasure, Annie. All thrilling things happen in their time." He grinned and shot her a wink.

They waded out into the stream and washed themselves. Walking back to dress, he suggested, "Tessa and her outlaw friends should have made it to the mine by now."

"What are you planning to do? There's at least eight of them. I can't believe Uncle Charlie would kill his own brother."

"Greed, Annie. It's happened before and it will happen again. You're lucky you didn't tell Tessa how to find Rainbow's End. She would have killed you."

"I believe she would have. That school changed Tessa. Made her evil."

He lifted her into her saddle, then got into his. They headed downstream. He asked, "Now that we're here and you know the truth about Tessa and her father, do you want to take possession of the mine? You can back out if you wish. There's still time. We can ride out of Henson's Creek and leave them to kill one another."

Annie didn't hesitate in answering, "I don't want them to have it. Uncle Charlie had my father killed. If that weren't enough, he also subjected me and four women and two girls to much humiliation and considerable physical and mental pain. Uncle Charlie has to pay for that. Tessa, too. Yes, I want the mine."

"You do realize it means killing the whole lot of them?"

"Yes. It's the least I can do to honor my father. Will you help me?"

"Of course. All of them deserve to die."

Annie sighed heavily now that the decision had been made. She asked, "How do we go about doing it? What's the plan?"

"Simple. We follow their tracks to the mine. God knows there will be plenty of them. It goes without saying, they will be waiting for us. Probably at the mine."

"Won't they see us coming and start shooting?"

"No. It will be pouring down rain. The rain will hide us. We'll walk in and be on them before they know it."

Coming even with the huge stone, they halted and faced the gulch beyond the creek. Fargo saw hoofprints where the outlaws had joined Tessa. The hoofprints led into the water, emerged on the other side, and headed straight as an arrow into the gulch. "I'll follow till my sixth sense warns me to halt, then we will dismount and wait for the rain." He nudged the Ovaro to walk and crossed to where the riders left the stream.

The Trailsman saw the riders had put their horses to gallop. He chuckled.

"Mr. Fargo, what's so funny?"

"Those big, bad men."

"Oh?"

He reined to a halt and motioned Annie to come alongside him. Pointing to hoofprints, he told her, "They came out of the water galloping. That tells me they're either afraid of our guns or they suddenly caught a severe case of gold fever. In any event, they now have much to lose. And that, my dear, will work to our advantage. That's why I chuckled."

"Our advantage? I don't understand, Mr. Fargo. They have us outnumbered, eight to two." Annie's shoulders sagged at her own arithmetic.

"Let me explain. First, are you afraid to die?"

"Out here? Now?"

"Yes. If we continue, then within the next few hours or so, it could happen to both of us."

Annie stared up the gulch a long moment before saying, "No, Mr. Fargo, I'm not afraid to die."

"Why do you say that?"

Turning to face him, she answered, "They killed my father and tried to kill me."

"Then what you're saying is, you seek revenge."

"I hadn't thought of it that way, but yes, I want revenge. Want it very badly."

"And the gold has nothing to do with it?"

"Of course not, Mr. Fargo. Why should it?"

"Because you can't serve two masters at the same time. In this case, revenge and gold. If you were drawn by the gold, you would be afraid to die, for fear of losing it. The emotion that spawns revenge at any cost, even if it means death, blots out everything else—in this case the prospect of gold. Revenge is powerful. That's what I meant when I said they have much to lose and it will work to our advantage.

"Revenge doesn't exist in their minds. The gold does. Right now, they are blinded by it. They are the ones who are afraid to die, because it would mean losing a fortune. And that means this, Annie: a small voice will make them think twice before shooting at us. It will be telling them that if they do, it will expose their position and we might kill them. That same quiet voice will tell them to be extra cautious, that it is better to stay alive and gun us down later, when we least expect it to happen."

"And that's why we must kill all of them," Annie muttered solemnly.

"That's right. Otherwise, you'd be looking over your shoulder forever, waiting for one or more of them to appear and shoot you."

"Uh, what happens after we kill them, Mr. Fargo? I don't know anything about mining for gold."

"I've thought about that also. I've decided to offer my help until the first snow flies, then take you back to Wagon Wheel Gap."

Annie's broad smile and the twinkle in her eyes conveyed more than words could say. Fargo proceeded following the hoofprints heading up the timbered gulch.

After going quite a distance, the hoofprints turned abruptly to the right. Fargo reined to a halt and looked for the marker—not that it made any difference. He spotted a short length of frayed hemp rope dangling from a branch of blue spruce. Shifting his gaze to the far side of the gulch, he studied the terrain. He didn't like what he saw. That side of the gulch was much more irregular than the side on which he stood. And it was barren of trees or any kind of covering undergrowth, but was covered by rocks, large and small. There was an abundance of places for a man to poke a rifle through. Fargo didn't know the distance to the mine. It could be close or far. Tracking them on a rocky surface would be difficult, impossible in a downpour. He glanced at the clouds and knew they'd better hurry on.

Handing Annie his Sharps, he asked her to give him her Smith & Wesson. "I'll ride ahead. You cover me with the rifle. If you see me get shot, you are to ride out of this gulch. Don't look back. Get the hell out of Henson's Creek. Work your way back to the Gap."

"No, Mr. Fargo. I'm here to kill . . . or die in the trying. I will protect your backside, but I won't run."

He looked and grinned at her. Fargo liked her spunk. Finally he said, "Wait here till I wave you forward." He stuck the Smith & Wesson in the back of his waistband.

She nodded; he nudged the Ovaro to walk.

As he approached a line of big boulders, his eyes were in constant movement, scanning for a rifle barrel. He halted the Ovaro when he heard several hammers being cocked and a hard masculine voice growl, "That's far enough, mister. Drop your gun. Don't come any closer or you're a dead man. We want to palaver with you."

Fargo drew his Colt slowly and dropped it. Neal Barrow's head appeared over a boulder. After looking at

Annie, he said, "There's enough gold for all of us, you two included. Why not let bygones be bygones?"

Before Fargo could speak, Tessa rose from behind another boulder and climbed atop it. When she did, Warren and Charlie exposed themselves. Tessa said, "Skye, darling, I told them not to kill you."

The Sharps barked. The impact of the bullet in Tessa's chest catapulted her off the boulder. Fargo wheeled the Ovaro and fell out of the saddle.

The loud retort of a .52 Spencer, fired from across the gulch, rent the humid air. Warren's head exploded.

Fargo scooped up his Colt and pulled the Smith & Wesson from his waistband. He lunged against the nearest boulder.

The Sharps and the Spencer, now joined by a Henry and another Spencer, laid down blistering firepower.

Fargo leapt boldly over the boulder. The outlaws were in retreat amid the hail of rifle fire. Fargo shot at near-point-blank range with both his weapons. Ray and John Barrow lurched forward. Blood blossomed between their shoulder blades as they fell onto the rocks.

Chance, the sole surviving bank robber, turned to shoot Fargo. The big man dropped him with one shot from the Colt. It bored a red hole in Chance's forehead.

Rifle fire knocked Frank Barrow down. He grabbed his bloody thigh and swung to fire at Fargo. Fargo blew his brains out with the Smith & Wesson.

Charlie Hogg and Neal Barrow scampered over boulders and out of sight. Fargo stalked them. He wounded Neal just when it started to rain. The deluge prevented him from getting off a second shot. Fargo reloaded his Colt and continued stalking in the direction he'd last seen them go.

After plodding quite a distance up the rocky slope, a large black hole loomed in the torrential downpour. Fargo dropped and crawled beside the dark, man-made hole. He shouted, "Come out, gents, and meet the devil himself face to face. I'm going to send your sorry asses to hell so you can meet him in person."

Three shots from within the mine answered.

Fargo sat with his back next to the entrance. After

sweating the renegades about half an hour, Annie stumbled up to him. Right behind her came Melba and Jonas. Then, Angus McCord's huge frame appeared in the rain. He was followed by Magee and, to Fargo's surprise, Doe's Tail and Blue Corn.

McCord shoved a bottle of bourbon into Fargo's waiting hands and grunted, "Compliments of Miss Candy. Don't care for the stuff myself." Angus nodded toward the entrance and asked, "How many you got holed up in there?"

Fargo warmed his insides with the amber liquid before telling him, "Two. How did you find me anyhow?"

Jonas answered, "Him and Magee paid a visit to Chief Fire Dances."

"Took along six horses to bribe him with," Magee chortled.

"Asked the chief to tell me where you was," Angus began. "He made me and Magee here guzzle that damn peyote with him. I ain't never again gonna partake of that stuff."

Magee picked up on the story. "Anyhow, the next morning he told us that we could find you under an upside-down rainbow, looking at it from the wrong side turned around. We thanked him for giving us a riddle and gave him the six horses. He gave us two back and told us to take his daughters, they were giving him a fit."

"We knew you were headed for the Gap," Angus said. "So we went there."

Jonas hurried to add, "I saw the four of them ride up and stop at Miss Candy's."

Melba said, "I heard Mr. McCord ask Miss Candy where you all went and remembered that Jonas had drawn a map of their butts. So I went and fetched Jonas."

"Anyhow," Angus began, "he and I, along with Magee here, we got our noggins together and pondered the map Jonas had drawn and what Fire Dances had told us. By damn, if Jonas didn't figure it out. Took four bottles of whiskey to do it."

Jonas popped his suspenders and said, "When they told me what the chief told 'em, at first it didn't make no sense to me. Then, by cracky, it slowly dawned on me what Fire Dances meant. I took the maps to the mirror ahind the bar, turned 'em upside down, and looked at 'em in the mirror. Then I thought about how they would look if I flipped 'em over. I knowed right then the mine was in Gunsmoke Gulch, right where I found those two nuggets that day that grizzly got me down on the bank of Henson's Creek."

"So we made a beeline for Gunsmoke Gulch," Magee said.

"I know all the shortcuts," McCord snorted. "After clearing Creede . . ." He paused to say, "You left dead men for them to haul off." He picked back up on what he was telling, "I took them to catch up with you—"

Fargo interrupted to ask, "What made you think I would find the mine, huh, McCord?"

McCord answered through a soft grin, "Because you're smart as ol' Billy Hell, Fargo. I was betting you'd figure out those maps, same as Jonas."

Fargo chuckled. "Go on with your tale, Angus."

"Isn't no tale," McCord corrected. "It's a fact. Anyhow, we arrived on the east side of Gunsmoke just in time to see you drop your Colt. That told us something bad was happening. When the little lady here—we couldn't see her from where we was—blowed that woman off the boulder, we started firing. You know the rest."

Fargo looked at Melba. "What are you doing here?"

She glanced at Jonas. Even through the rain on her face Fargo saw her blush. "Aw, golly, Fargo, me and Jonas are gonna get married after all this is over. I love him and he loves me back."

Annie suggested to Jonas, "Seeing as how you found those first two nuggets, what would you say if I asked you to help me work the mine?" She quickly added, "As a full partner, of course."

Jonas stuck his hand in hers. Grinning, he shook it and said, "I'd say you got yourself a deal. Now, while I've seen your ass, I don't know my partner's name."

"Annie Hogg. And I don't want you looking at my ass again, partner."

Fargo stood and looked at the opening and then at the

sky. "You men want to rush them now, or wait till it's good and dark?"

Jonas and Magee shrugged. McCord grunted, "Get it over with."

Thumbing the hammer of his Colt to cocked position, Fargo told the women to stay clear of the entrance to the mine, then said to Magee, "You and I are going to give them something to worry about. You want to run to the far side of this black hole first, or have me do it?"

Magee said he would go first. When Magee got set to run, Fargo poked his Colt around the edge of the opening and nodded. Magee's legs moved like pistons. He was halfway across the entrance before the outlaws could react and fire. Fargo emptied the Colt to pin them down. Magee made it to the other side unscathed.

McCord covered for Fargo, who emptied the Smith & Wesson during the short run. After reloading his Colt, Fargo nodded to McCord that he was ready. Because the two men inside had seen them dart across the opening and were probably still watching that side, Fargo motioned for McCord to launch the attack.

McCord went in firing. An instant later, Fargo swung around the edge with his Colt belching hot lead. He glimpsed Annie follow Jonas inside. Magee was right behind Fargo.

All five dived to the floor of the mine to leave the smallest silhouettes possible. A barrage of bullets sailed over their bodies. Fargo quickly reloaded.

Boots scuffed on the hard ground. The culprits were taking up new positions.

"Leave Uncle Charlie for me," Annie called to the others.

Fargo whispered to Magee for him to roll to the center of the mine shaft and fire one shot. Magee rolled and fired. Fargo shielded his left eye with his hand. During the flickering of the gun's muzzle flash, Fargo spotted enough of Neal Barrow's face to put a bullet in it.

Fargo told Magee to keep firing. "Okay, ma'am, Charlie's all yours," Fargo called to Annie.

"Wait a minute," Charlie shouted. "I didn't mean for Roscoe or Annie to get killed."

They heard running feet coming toward them. Fargo and McCord fired so Annie could see her target. Charlie sped past them. He made it to just outside the opening before the Sharps barked. Charlie grabbed for the searing hot slug that drilled into his back. His legs folded and he fell facedown. Annie stepped to the entrance, pointed the Sharps at him, and blew a hunk of his head off.

"Goddamn, I got me a mean partner," Jonas muttered.

Fargo went to her and took her in his arms. Looking at the other women, he told them to come in out of the rain.

They stayed in the mine that night. Doe's Tail found the two bags of bank money. After morning coffee all but the new partners and Melba rode away in the mist.

Where Henson's Creek joined the Gunnison, Fargo looked behind. A spectacular rainbow arched over Gunsmoke Gulch.

He mumbled, "Peace and tranquillity."

Angus McCord asked, "What did you say?"

"I said these bags of money are heavy."